Big Island Remembered
[LARGE PRINT]

Rollercoasters, Romance & Rage on Lake Minnetonka

Bette Hammel & Reed Wahlberg

Copyright © 2020 Reed Wahlberg
All rights reserved.
ISBN: 9798648252714

Table of Contents

Notes to readers 1
Prologue 2
Excelsior – Summer 1899 ... 3
Macie & Mr. Jerome 8
Mississippi 14
River Reflections 21
Arrival, July 11, 1899 27
Beginnings 35
Backstories 44
Challenges 54
Dinner Guests 57
Town Talk 64
Decisions 72
Keith 82
Confidantes 89
Progress 95
Tea 99
The Grand Ball 107
Big Island 112
Nighttime 119
Joy 124
Observations 128

Floating 135
Bells 139
Requiem 143
Adventure 150
Discussion 157
Wayzata 162
St. Paul 174
Collaboration 202
Grandmother 213
St. Mary's 223
Questions 241
Zunker Photography 246
Puzzles 256
Searching Anew 266
Clippings 275
Blooming 279
Celebrating 282
Acknowledgements 297
About the authors 304
Bibliography 310
Endnotes 316

Notes to readers

As evidenced by the bibliography, much of this cozy mystery is based on historically accurate information about life in Excelsior, Minnesota, at the turn of the 20th century. However, this book is first and foremost a novel. Timelines have been stretched to enhance the plot, the majority of which is fictitious. This book is not intended to serve as a scholarly work yet endnotes are provided at the back of the book to distinguish some of the fact from the fiction. Those notes also provide other historical tidbits to enhance the reader's experience.

Prologue

In the myths of time, a fabled lake was discovered in Minnesota hidden from the white man; "Minn-ni-tanka," certain native Americans softly whispered its name. Numerous publications recorded its history until its reputation had grown well beyond Minnesota, even to large cities such as Kansas City, Cedar Rapids and New Orleans.

Excelsior – Summer 1899

The first hints of sun illuminate the tops of the trees along the southeastern shore of Lake Minnetonka, about 14 miles due west of Minneapolis. The few towns scattered along the 125 miles of shoreline on the big lake are just coming alive. A very distant train whistle signals an impending arrival across the lake in Wayzata. Puffy clouds reflect perfectly in the water on this beautiful summer morning. Most of the shores, still pristine and untouched by man, are inhabited by a great diversity of wildlife. Deer drink at water's edge. Beavers bask in the early sunshine atop their lodge. Periodic loon calls punctuate the near perfect silence from afar. A set of gentle waves signal the earlier passage of a steamer from Excelsior. Those waves cause the lifeless body to rise and fall among the reeds lining the shore.

Macie & Mr. Jerome

In St. Louis, Missouri, the temperature was 103 degrees on June 28, 1899, as Macie, a lithe young Southern woman blessed with wavy golden blonde hair, bent over her employer's legal papers. She was proud to be bookkeeper for Sir Will Jerome[1], a distinguished Civil War captain. As a Missourian, he had denounced slavery. He now had loyal blacks[2] on his staff and was widely recognized as a successful land grant attorney and developer. The spirited Mr. Jerome, known for his traditional short grey beard, and wearing a cool white shirt and summer-weight suit, came bounding into the office. "Macie," he cried, "I'm getting out of this hot place and heading up North. I know Minnesota is cool country with the most wonderful lake where I've built a grand hotel plus a summer home for my family. I think you know it, Northome."

"Yes, you've mentioned how much your children love being there -- all six of them," smiled Macie.

"We're late going up there this summer, but I have important new business to tend to. I'm investing in building an amusement park on an island in the middle of that lake, Lake Minnetonka," he said.

"I've never heard of an amusement park on an island," she replied.

"Yes, it's pretty rare. It also presents some building challenges." After a brief pause, he continued. "I've been meaning to ask you something, Macie. I could really use your help up in Minnesota. Is there any chance that you could work for me there for at least a few months?"

"Really! I'm honored that you feel that I could help."

"Of that, there is no doubt."

"What would my responsibilities include?"

"The hotel has lost its bookkeeper. I would like you to take over the bookkeeping until they find a permanent replacement. I could also really use your help tracking the finances with this new Lake Minnetonka park project."

While she may have doubted her abilities to help him to the degree that he envisioned, she, like everyone else he encountered, had full confidence in him. With his keen mind and genial smile, he was a born leader, much admired by everyone. If Mr. Jerome felt that she was up to the task, she would certainly give it her all.

"How would I get there?" she asked.

"I need to be up there by July 13th for an important meeting about the proposed amusement park. You could take the train and get there quickly, along with some members of my staff and new recruits to work at the hotel. However, my wife and I wanted to make the trip more of a vacation. We're leaving by steamboat Thursday. We would love to have you join us on the boat. Since none of our children will be traveling with us this year, you could be our token 'child' for the trip."

"That sounds wonderful! I've never been on a steamboat. Where would I live up there?"

"There is a nice boarding house in the town near the shore of Lake Minnetonka. I know the couple who run it. They do a great job and would make your stay very comfortable. I hope you don't mind but I've already contacted them to secure lodging for you."

Macie liked the sound of Mr. Jerome's plan as she mulled over the whole situation.

After a moment to let her think, he continued. "So, what do you think? Will this work for you?"

"Actually, I think this will work very well. I had just started looking for a new place to live. The timing on your proposal is just about perfect. There is nothing holding me back. Plus, the work sounds interesting! I am thrilled to accept your proposal!"

"Wonderful!"

"Thank you for your confidence in me, Mr. Jerome. This sounds like a great adventure!"

"Thank you in advance for your help, Macie. I'm sure you will love Minnesota."

When Macie departed the office, she rushed off to her apartment to start packing. "What in the world am I going to wear in Minnesota?" she wondered. "That's cold country." Not that she had much to choose from with her daily selection of cool muslin tops and calico skirts. She owned only one soft pale cotton sweater and one navy blue jacket that would probably be okay for this trip. She twirled girlishly around the room imagining what fun might be in store for her during this adventure.

Mississippi

Early in the afternoon, Mr. and Mrs. Jerome and Macie joined with about 200 other lightly dressed folks in boarding the *Samuel Clemens* steamboat in St. Louis, bound for St. Paul. All were enthused about adventure and anxious to escape the oppressive summer heat. The three-decker paddlewheeler had a special glamorous lure for Macie, with its tall chimneys, long white decks and the sound of music frequently emanating from within. As she boarded, she recalled reading Mark Twain's book about steamboating on the river when he wrote: *Steamboats are like wedding cakes without the complications.*[4] "He certainly had captured the romance of steamboats," she thought, "and now I get to experience one for myself!"

Before departing St. Louis, Mr. Jerome had warned his wife and

Macie that while the voyage was slated for five days, they had to be prepared for the possibility that the trip could go longer. They were traveling fairly late in the season when the river level was likely to be a bit lower. There was always the possibility of the boat getting hung up on a sandbar, which could result in an extensive delay.

They spent the first day getting settled into their cabins, exploring the boat and its amenities and watching the world glide by. Macie was happy to finally have the chance to get better acquainted with Mr. Jerome's wife. Christine Jerome, a pert, vivacious woman in her early 50's was well known for her beaming smile and great sense of humor. As the well-educated wife of the esteemed attorney, she was highly regarded in St. Louis society circles. Macie found her to be a pleasant conversationalist and they spent a lot of time chatting that afternoon.

Shortly after dinner on their first evening aboard ship, Macie and the Jeromes entered the dining room again and sat down. The captain had already started his nightly talk. They were immediately struck by the aura of professionalism and confidence around the captain. He was wearing a navy-blue double-breasted jacket with 3 stripes on his cuff. His grey beard suggested his age and his significant boat piloting experience. "Steamboating has changed a lot over the past century," he said. "You folks are fortunate. I hope that you are finding your accommodations suitable. That was likely not the case 50-60 years ago. Back then, the boat was more like a floating dormitory packed with bunkbeds."

"Sorry. Not for me!" Mrs. Jerome whispered under her breath.

The captain took a sip of water, giving the audience time to think about their comfortable private cabins with colorful pillows for accent on the beds.

"I hope you enjoyed your dinner this evening. I think you will find the meals on board to be very good. In the early days of steamboating the food in the cafeteria was notorious for being barely edible. At every stop, passengers would scurry ashore to find their own food to bring aboard for the next leg of the trip." Thoughts of some in the audience likely turned to the delicious dinner they had just enjoyed featuring blackened catfish, au gratin potatoes and candied carrots served on fine china with silver. Other audience members looked around again at the lovely dining room featuring large windows, dark wood paneling, Persian rugs, and chandeliers.

"You folks are also benefitting greatly from a big change in our boat engines," the captain continued. "They used to be much noisier and they created more vibration and heat. That heat, noise and vibration made sleeping difficult."

"That would not have been much of a vacation," Mrs. Jerome whispered quickly to her husband.

"I'll cover more of the history of steamboating in later talks." The captain paused, then continued. "This trip will feature major stops at Hannibal, Dubuque, LaCrosse and Red Wing. I would encourage you to get off the boat at every opportunity to do some exploring. At some stops, we will offer optional shore excursions. For example, you could learn about how rifle ammunition is made by joining our visit to the shot tower in Dubuque."[5]

"I definitely want to do that one," Mr. Jerome whispered aloud.

"In LaCrosse, an expert on Mississippi mussels and the pearl button manufacturing industry will come aboard our boat. If you are interested in buttons and how they are made, this lecture will be for you."

"I think I'll skip that one," Mr. Jerome commented to his wife.

"No, you won't, Dear. You'll be sitting right next to me, right?" she asked, smiling.

"How about taking a carriage ride down the crookedest road in the entire world?" the captain asked. "That's right. It is also very steep. Join us for a ride on Snake Alley in Burlington, Iowa." [6]

"I'm not missing that!" Macie exclaimed.

"Those are just a few of the things you'll be able to enjoy over the next few days. We will keep you informed about opportunities all along the way."

The captain paused momentarily, then continued.

"On behalf of the entire crew of the *Clemens*, I want to wish all of you a wonderful trip." With that, the captain doffed his hat and bowed.

A vigorous round of applause sounded as the captain left the hall. Spirited discussions of the wonderful adventures to come could be overheard throughout the room as people started to head back to their cabins for the night.

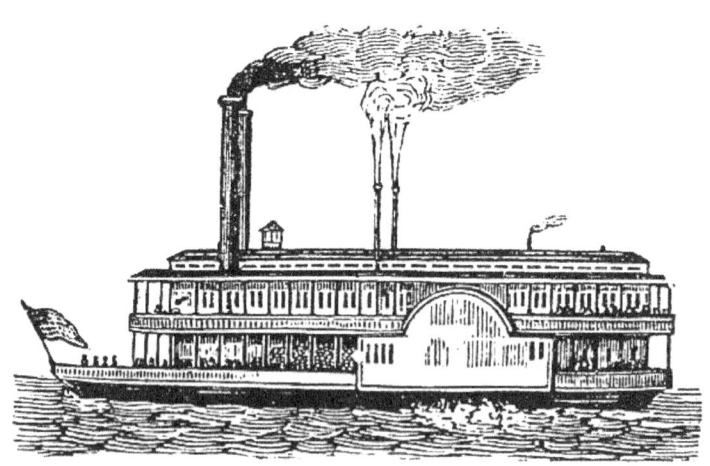

River Reflections

As they had done frequently during their journey, the Jeromes and Macie sat in the front of the ship on their favorite chairs with very slanted backs. On this, the final morning of their voyage, they were sipping tea while lazily watching the world glide by. As the *Clemens* had churned up the Mississippi, they had often marveled at the diversity in the scenery both along the shore and on the river itself. Large expanses of the shoreline were untouched by man and they spotted many types of birds and animals that live near the life-sustaining water. Most of the forest lands along the river contained young trees since, as the captain had pointed out in one of his talks, most of the old-growth trees had been logged during the earlier part of the century to fuel the steamboats. Now that coal was the primary steamboat fuel, the forests were starting to grow again. Every so often, a town would come into view. On occasion, homes reflected substantial wealth with sizeable windows, wide-open porches and glorious flower gardens. More commonly, homes were small and functional, providing basic shelter from the elements. Other steamboats were encountered often, most hauling freight but also a few with passengers headed downstream.

    One such steamboat headed downriver was approaching this morning. Macie looked up to the bridge where she could see the captain pulling down on a cord. As he did, billowing clouds of steam started exiting from the whistle device above the bridge. Eventually, even larger clouds emerged, and finally the wail of the whistle resonated across the river. The steamboat approaching from upriver then sounded its whistle.

"Have either of you figured out the whistling? I know that the two boats are communicating but I can't figure out when they whistle once or twice," Mrs. Jerome said.

"Have you noticed that our boat always whistles first?" Mr. Jerome replied. "That's because the boat going upriver signals first to a boat going downriver. One blast by the boat going upriver means 'keep to the right.' Two blasts mean 'keep to the left.' A single blast in reply from the boat going downriver indicates agreement with the plan. I know that the captains can signal other things as well but that's as much I know."

"Ah. Interesting. Thanks, Dear," Mrs. Jerome replied.

As they were approaching the end of their journey to St. Paul, the thoughts of the Jeromes and Macie this morning turned wistful, focusing on some of the many highlights of their voyage.

"I'm going to miss the unique experience of just being on the boat, the gentle swaying while sleeping at night, the constant hum of the powerful engines," Mrs. Jerome noted.

"I have thoroughly enjoyed the singalongs around the piano," Macie replied. "I've never done more singing in my life."

"Agreed. The music aboard has been wonderful," Mr. Jerome said.

"And think about the interesting things we've seen and done along the way," Mrs. Jerome continued. "I found the lock and canal at Keokuk fascinating. What an incredible improvement for river travel! I enjoyed watching the whole process."[7]

"I agree," Macie nodded.

"I also found it stunning to think of the olden days before the construction of that canal and lock. To think that they would have to unload all the passengers and cargo, move everything over land up the river past the rapids, then reload everyone and everything on a second boat for the next stage of the voyage. Oh, my!" Mrs. Jerome shook her head in disbelief.

"I enjoyed all of our shore excursions," Macie noted.

"Me too," Mrs. Jerome replied. "Exploring Davenport was particularly fun."

"Surprisingly, one of my favorite experiences was the lecture on the pearl mussel button manufacturing industry in LaCrosse," Macie noted. "I had never known that they punched sections from the shells to make buttons."

"I thought that would be boring as sin," Mr. Jerome commented. "Sorry, Dear," turning to his wife. "You were right. It would have been a mistake to miss that lecture."

"And, Dear, a necklace featuring Mississippi mussel pearls would make a perfect memento from this wonderful vacation," Mrs. Jerome hinted, smiling and patting her husband lovingly on the hand.

The gentle rocking of the boat this morning was mesmerizing, and many passengers were dozing off. The Jeromes announced it was nap time and left for their cabin. Macie stayed put and reopened the book that she had been reading.

Later that day, the big steamer docked at St. Paul where they were quickly escorted by carriage to the ornate, gothic-inspired Ryan Hotel. The next day they joined with the rest of Mr. Jerome's workers, just arrived by train from St. Louis. Together they boarded a train headed for Deephaven, site of the St. Louis Hotel.

Arrival, July 11, 1899

Word that Will Jerome, the esteemed St. Louis attorney and real estate investor, who had developed the aristocratic St. Louis Hotel, was coming to Excelsior soon reached the local newspaper, the *Excelsior Journal*. Journal reporter and photographer, Buzz Greenfield knew all the local business gossip floating around and felt the future looked good for the thriving town. New development bringing people to town meant it would become a livelier place.

Recently, Buzz had previewed Jerome's new hotel, the St. Louis, and published a story about its luxurious features. He had described it as one of the most complete resort hotels in the Northwest, with two-story verandas affording every guest sweeping views of the beautiful lake below. Buzz rambled on in his story, "the whole place looks handsome, complete with marble-topped dressers, indoor plumbing, even a 'bathing room' in every unit." With 200 private rooms accommodating 400 guests, the hotel soon attracted trainloads of wealthy southern families from their overheated cities. The hotel, sometimes known as the Southern Aristocracy of the Northwest, was also among the first on the lake to offer new technology: a telephone[8] in the lobby. From St. Paul, travelers could board either the James J. Hill train, (the Great Northern) and transfer at Wayzata to a ferry boat or take the Milwaukee direct to the hotel in Deephaven. Mr. Jerome's party was taking the Milwaukee.

"We're getting close now," Mr. Jerome announced to Macie as the train ground to a halt in Minnetonka Mills.

Macie was surprised to see many blacks getting off the train there.

"I'll be right back," Mr. Jerome said as he quickly stood up and headed for the door of the train car. "Sam," he shouted, "have all of our workers get back on the train. We're not at the hotel yet."

Sam, a strapping young black man, replied: "But, Mr. Jerome, this is the colored stop. We were told that we were to get off here and walk to the hotel."[9]

"There will be no more of that, Sam. Have everyone hold up a second."

Mr. Jerome spotted the conductor and walked briskly towards him. After a brief discussion, Mr. Jerome turned again toward the foreman of his crew. "Have everyone get back on the train, Sam. The next stop is the one for our hotel and that's where we'll all get off."

Mr. Jerome shook his head as he retook his seat next to his wife and across from Macie. "We've won the war and ratified the 13th amendment a long time ago but this country still has far to go."

"That was a nice thing for you to do, Dear," Mrs. Jerome replied.

They resumed their watch out the window.

The next stop was for Deephaven. Macie and the Jeromes got off the train and boarded a tallyho, a small but fast horse-drawn wagon,[10] for the short ride to the hotel. Alighting from the wagon, Macie couldn't help shouting, "It's cool here! We're going to love Minnesota." Another passenger agreed, noting "it must be only 80 degrees."

When the St. Louis Hotel came into view, Macie was overjoyed. "What a fine-looking building! You must be mighty proud of your hotel, Mr. Jerome."

"Indeed, I am, Macie," he replied.

"And look down below," she exclaimed. "I see the lake you told us about: Lake Minnetonka. It's huge ... just breathtaking!"

A man with a camera approached the group and said "Excuse me, Mr. Jerome. Would you mind pausing a moment. I'd like to take a photograph of you there with your new hotel in the background."

"Mr. Greenfield, right? Sure, I'd be happy to oblige," turning so that Buzz was able to get an appropriate picture. "You're heading back to Excelsior, aren't you?

"I am," Buzz replied.

"Any chance that you could escort my bookkeeper, Macie, to Excelsior as she will be staying at the Olson boarding house there."

"Sure, I'd be happy to," Buzz replied.

"Macie, I've met Buzz on several trips up here. He's a nice gentleman and an excellent reporter and photographer. He'll get you to the boarding house safely," Mr. Jerome added.

Buzz Greenfield, a tall, genial fellow sporting an athletic build and a shock of light brown hair, picked up Macie's bags and pointed the direction. "Right this way, Miss Macie. We have a launch down there. It's a short ride to Excelsior."

As they walked across the grounds, Macie noted several small groups of men sitting in the shade, most of whom appeared to be talking and smoking cigars. She also noted several women dressed in their finery, languishing in the sun on the verandas of Mr. Jerome's hotel. She was surprised when they came across a large black woman sitting in the shade, nursing two white babies.[11]

Buzz could sense Macie's curiosity. "It's fairly common for the guests of the hotel to employ wet-nurses," he noted.

Shortly thereafter, they reached the dock down the hill. As she clambered aboard the comfortable large launch, Macie looked delighted. "Do you think someone here would teach me how to use one of these boats?" Macie said, smiling.

Buzz looked at her approvingly. "Well, you know around here, men usually drive these boats, especially the big ferry boats you see cruising by with lots of passengers. But I could teach you how to use a rowboat." Grinning, Buzz decided he and Macie would get along well. As a married man and father of two boys, he had taught lots of young people about boating and fishing. "We even have rowboat races."

"That sounds like fun," Macie replied.

"If you'd like, I'd be happy to take you to see the sights in town tomorrow morning."

"Sure! Thanks for the offer."

Upon arriving at the reddish-clad clapboard boarding house, the owners, Mr. and Mrs. Clem Olson, greeted Macie warmly. Macie felt a surge of happiness on meeting Mrs. Olson, a cheery older woman, with a motherly air. Giving Macie a big hug she said, "After all that travel, you must be famished. I have a nice bowl of vegetable soup for you in the kitchen. And, if it's all right with you, we would love to have you join us for dinner tomorrow night. I've invited some of our friends over. They would love to meet you and it would give you a chance to get acquainted with our community."

"That sounds wonderful!" Macie replied as they started to carry her bags upstairs.

Beginnings

Up early with excitement, Macie jumped into her regular clothes, a simple white muslin blouse over a print cotton skirt reaching the top of her boots, grabbed her little blue hat and headed out the door. She had about twenty minutes to spare before she was scheduled to meet with Buzz to tour the town. She decided to have a cup of coffee at Hardy's café, which she had noticed just down the block from the boarding house. Entering the café, she saw that all the tables were occupied. There was a small counter with one empty spot where she sat down. As she did, the woman sitting next to her spoke up.

"Good morning!" the woman said.

Macie turned and smiled. This middle-aged woman looked unlike the women Macie had seen at this point in town. She had a glamorous look about her, wearing quite a bit of makeup and dressed accordingly in a bright pink gown trimmed with ruffled white sleeves. Her dark brown hair was swept up on her head with an antique hair comb.

"Good morning!" Macie replied. "It's a lovely morning, isn't it?"

"It certainly is. Will you be able to take advantage of this beautiful weather?"

"Actually, yes! I'm going to tour the town with the photographer for the local newspaper."

"That should be delightful! You must be new to Excelsior."

"That's true. I just arrived yesterday from St. Louis."

Macie requested a cup of coffee from the waitress.

"What brings you to this little town all the way from St. Louis?"

"I'm working as a bookkeeper for Will Jerome. He's a top attorney and developer who specializes in building projects. He built the St. Louis Hotel in Deephaven, for example."

"Ah, yes, I've heard about that hotel. It's supposed to be spectacular."

"How about you? Have you lived in Excelsior a long time?"

"Actually, I'm just spending the summer here. I'm from St. Paul and I'm on vacation."

"How are you keeping yourself busy while you're here?"

"Oh, I've been having a nice time. I've got several little projects underway."

"What kind of projects?"

"I've been writing some essays, generally reflections on my life." Then, lowering her voice a bit so as not to be overheard, she added: "Just between the two of us, I like to sip some good wine while I write. It stimulates my creativity."

"Is that legal? I think Mr. Jerome mentioned that this is a dry town."

"There are many people in this town who could benefit from some wine. They're too uptight about too many things. A little hooch never hurt anyone, and it can add some enjoyment to life – and I do enjoy life!"

Macie smiled.

"My newest passion is drawing. I knew an artist one time in my life. She knew I was creative and taught me how to begin sketching. So, I've been having fun sketching some of the children I've seen playing here in Excelsior. I'm not very good yet, but my goal is to improve."

"Interesting!"

"I'd be happy to show you some of my creations."

"That would be wonderful!"

"Come on over to my place anytime. I have a little apartment above the hardware store. I must warn you, however," smiling again and lowering her voice almost to a whisper, "sipping wine also increases the enjoyment of looking at sketches."

Macie laughed. "I must run now. It's been great chatting with you. Sorry but I didn't introduce myself. I'm Macie Stewart," extending her hand to shake.

"Delighted to meet you, Miss Macie Stewart! I'm Meranda Delaquila. I hope to see you soon. Have fun on your tour of Excelsior."

"Thanks!" Macie set two pennies on the counter then was off to find Buzz down at the docks.

As Macie left, she thought "Gee, I've just met my first older woman here and I didn't even think of her age. She seems so full of life." Macie quickly located Buzz at dockside where she perched on a railing and breathed in the sunshine. There, where the water rippled right up to the shore, Macie felt the impact of this new environment--the crisp refreshing air, the enormous forests, the boundless lake breathing a welcome. What a change from St. Louis!

Buzz understood. "You bet, Macie, there's something magic about living by this mighty lake. And you'll soon see how much we love boating. My buddies and I row out to the islands, race each other and bring our fishing tackle along. This is a great fishing lake. And our wives like it when we bring home fresh walleyes or bass for supper. It's fun."

They headed out on their tour, starting up the boardwalk along Water Street, which was lined with a hodgepodge of small, mostly wood-frame buildings. Already the town had many facilities such as a barber shop, livery stable, hardware store, bakery, general store, bank, jail house, post office, railroad depot, plus several rooming houses and cafes. A taller brick building known as the Lodge offered room for offices, plus more space for the mayor's office and council chambers.

The three-story Excelsior school house was built on another street and featured a more distinguished architecture using Chaska yellow brick. It was plain to see that the town was flourishing.

Macie asked: "Who built these buildings here on Water Street?"

Buzz, acting as tour guide, quickly replied, "Oh, I think Charlie Miller did a lot. He started out as a carpenter but over time found he could actually detail a building too. So, he wound up calling himself a 'Master Builder.' I happen to like his work."

They turned left onto 2nd Street after waiting for a wagon to pass that was being driven at breakneck speed by a very young man. The horse appeared to be running all out.

"Hey, there!" Buzz yelled as the wagon passed in front of them. "You're gonna kill someone!" Turning to Macie, he said, "Pretty ridiculous, huh?"

Macie, shaking her head, noted, "I can't imagine what is so urgent." Then pausing momentarily, she continued. "What about churches, Buzz?" Macie queried. "I thought Excelsior was noted for churches of many faiths."

"You're right," replied Buzz. Our town was founded by religious folks who came from the East." As they walked, he pointed out churches and schools that were built on either side of the main street. "The earliest church was Trinity Episcopal. It's noted for its outstanding architecture using local stone."

"How about that one?" Macie asked, pointing at another church building further up the street.

"That's the First Congregational Church of Excelsior. That's the Reverend Charles Galpin's church. He was one of our pioneers who founded Excelsior on these high bluffs. And just look at that tall spire on his church. Like it? The

Methodists have a church too. All the towns surrounding the lake have a variety of denominations."

They continued their walk through the hilly town as far as the beach off the Commons, an elevated area at the tip of Excelsior Bay. Macie now realized how different Excelsior looked compared to St. Louis, the latter a large city and the former a small town. Excelsior's population had now swelled to 700-some people, not counting the annual summer visitors of which there were many during this, the peak season. Macie smiled as she noted a posted sign that read,

Shooting and Hitching Horses to trees on these grounds is strictly forbidden.

Backstories

Macie thanked Buzz for showing her around the town. She then headed back to the boarding house for a brief discussion with Mrs. Olson and, from there, took off for Meranda's apartment.

"Macie!" exclaimed Meranda after opening the door. "Good to see you. Come on in."

Macie entered and immediately saw sketches covering the dining room table.

"As you can see, I've been doing some drawing down at Commons Beach. Could I interest you in a glass of wine? I've also got some hot water in the kettle if you'd prefer a cup of tea."

"Ooohh, a cup of tea sounds good. Thanks!"

Macie hovered over the sketches as Meranda poured her tea. "These are nice!" Macie exclaimed. Children were clearly Meranda's favorite subject as most of the sketches focused on children at play. She had several other drawings posted on her walls.

"Thanks. I try but I'm really having fun with drawing. Have a seat and make yourself comfortable," pulling out two cozy-looking chairs around a little table. Macie sat down in one while Meranda took the other. "So, did you have a nice tour?"

"I did. Cute little town! I know that I'm gonna like spending the summer here. By the way, that's a beautiful scarf!"

Meranda reached for a corner of the scarf that she was wearing around her neck to display its lavender blue colors accented with yellow and red flowers. "Thanks. I love this. It was a gift from a dear friend of mine in St. Paul. It was made in Tahiti. I wear it at home anytime I want to perk up my feelings. The only time I wear it outside is on the rare occasion that I'm paying a visit to a man who has piqued my curiosity," Meranda added, smiling and winking. "So, Miss Macie. Tell me more about yourself. I'd love to hear your life story."

"Unfortunately, that life story is not such a pleasant one, I must warn you."

"Well, if you'd care to share, I'm all ears. I'm pretty empathetic as my story also has some unfortunate twists and turns."

"I was born Macie Newman on a farm near Florissant, Missouri. My parents were farmers. Unfortunately, they were killed in a housefire when I was a baby."

"Oh, mon Dieu!" Meranda replied. "That's awful!"

"According to my relatives, they were a wonderful couple who were extremely hard working but relatively poor. They were thrilled about having me."

"I'm so sorry, Macie."

"I ended up being adopted soon after the fire. My adoptive parents, who I refer to as my 'stepparents,' are quite wealthy so I grew up in a very comfortable home. I adored my stepmother and the years with her were some of the happiest of my life. Unfortunately, she died of cancer when I was twelve."

"What about your stepfather?" Meranda asked.

"My stepfather is a very successful real estate developer. Some small towns just west of St. Louis boomed under his leadership in attracting lots of wealthy families. What's more, my stepfather created several championship golf courses."

"Yep, I've heard some of my men friends mention golf. Apparently, it's a growing sport."

"My stepfather's a workaholic. But, in his free time, he can be found on the golf course. He never really showed much interest in me at all.

He seems to care much more about his golf game than he does about me."

"Do you have an active relationship with him?" sipping her Chardonnay.

"Not really. After my stepmother died, he shipped me off to boarding school. I came back home from time to time but the lack of love at home was depressing. Eventually I quit going back home at all. He doesn't really encourage me either."

"I'm sorry. You were right. You've had a tough childhood. However, it's clear to me, Macie, that you're resilient. There must have been other people in your life who nurtured you along."

"Yes, both sets of my biological grandparents have played huge roles in my life. I visited them whenever possible. Unfortunately, only my paternal grandmother is still living. She's still down in Florissant, the closest town to where I was born.

Recently, she came across some old photos of my biological parents and just sent them to me."

"I'd be very interested to see them."

"Okay, I'll bring them over sometime soon."

"Formidable!"

"In thinking further about my stepfather, I have to admit he's been a generous financial provider for me. He sent me to top schools where the instructors were generally incredible. I have many lifelong friends from those schools, both fellow students and instructors. They've given me tremendous support over the years. And Mr. Jerome, the attorney that I'm working for, has been outstanding. He treats me almost like a member of his family."

Macie paused to sip generously from her tea. "So how about you, Meranda. What's your story?"

"I was born and raised in New Orleans. I had a fairly normal middle-class childhood. I was always somewhat rebellious, so I left home pretty early on. I was really intrigued by the Mississippi River so, at age 18, I took a steamship all the way up the river to St. Paul."

"We just made that same trip up the river to St. Paul from St. Louis."

"I found some odd jobs there and never left. I've always been pretty good in managing money. With the money I saved, I eventually bought a house, rented out some of my rooms and kept on saving. Eventually, I owned several properties. I've had some troubles with certain tenants over the years, but I have to say I'm pretty proud of how well I've done."

"Do you still have family back in New Orleans?"

"No, I don't. Both of my parents are gone. They were both only children themselves, so I have no immediate relatives."

"I've heard you exclaiming at times in a foreign language. French?"

"Yes. Mom's parents immigrated from France. We always spoke French in their presence. A lot of people in New Orleans still speak French. There are times where French just comes out of my mouth instinctively. I hope that's not a problem."

"No, that's all right. It sounds exotic. You married?"

"No. Never have been. I've had several significant relationships, but I never felt the urge to settle on one man. And some of those relationships led to real pain. I'm still open to other possibilities, if you know what I mean." Meranda winked again. "How about you? Is there a significant man in your life?"

"No," replied Macie, pausing momentarily. "I don't think you've recounted the 'unfortunate twists and turns' you mentioned earlier."

"Oh, we'll save those stories for another day. For now, let's just say that I'm hoping to turn over a new leaf in some of the ways that I lead my life."

"Fair enough. Well, this has been fun, Meranda. I really enjoy talking with you."

"I feel the same," she replied.

"I actually stopped by to invite you to a little dinner party that the owners of the boarding house where I'm staying, the Olsons, are hosting tonight."

"You're staying at a boarding house and the hosts are inviting you to their dinner party? That sounds like pretty unusual hospitality for a boarder."

"I think I'm benefitting from their long-term relationship with Mr. Jerome. I know he made all arrangements with them for me."

"Ahh..."

"Anyway, I asked if I could invite my new friend and Mrs. Olson replied, 'Absolutely.' It'll start at seven."

"That sounds terrific. I know where to find that boarding house. I'll be there. Thanks for thinking of me."

"Sure thing. Well, I'm headed to the office now for my first day of work. It should be interesting! See you tonight," she added, heading out the door to catch a boat to her office at the hotel.

Challenges

Mr. Jerome was not at the hotel this morning, so Macie was led to her little office by the hotel manager, Mr. Adams, a balding and bespectacled man, a couple inches shorter than Macie. "I apologize for the unkempt state of this office," he said, admitting that handling of documents was not a skill that he or anyone else at the hotel possessed. "Unfortunately, even the previous bookkeeper was apparently not very good at it either. Please let me know if I can assist you with any questions that you have in the days and weeks to come. I know that this is going to be somewhat challenging." With that, he wished her luck and left her.

After settling in a bit, Macie sat back and examined the setting. This small room did not share the luxurious feel of the rest of the hotel. No mahogany paneling had been installed here. Macie guessed that the room had originally been intended only for storage. The walls were plastered and painted a dull gray. They were bare except for a calendar. One side of the room contained filing cabinets. Fortunately, the room had a large window facing west that allowed lots of natural light into the room.

    Macie approached the window and gazed wistfully down toward the lake below. She decided that one of her first tasks would be to improve the organization of the workspace. Mr. Jerome had prepared her for this. Apparently, the folks at the front desk of the hotel were doing well in handling the day-to-day transactions involving the hotel guests. However, some of the higher-level business transactions of the hotel had been neglected over the past year or so. As a result, a variety of documents including invoices, receipts, bank records and others had been accumulating in piles on the desk that she now occupied.

Macie knew that this chaos had to be tamed. This was going to take some time and effort, but she knew the end result would be satisfying. She also knew that she would learn a lot about running a hotel via this process.

"It feels good to have some real work to do," she thought. "And to think that I get to do that work with this beautiful lake just down the hill. Life is good!" With that, she grabbed the first stack of documents and set about sorting them into logical piles.

Dinner Guests

The evening began with Mr. and Mrs. Olson politely welcoming guests into their home for dinner. Mrs. Olson was happy that her dining room had space for a long rectangular-shaped table that could hold almost 20 people. Macie was excited to meet these Excelsior residents. She was obviously the youngest person in the room and met them all, graciously repeating their names so she would remember. Buzz was there to help her out. And Macie was pleased to meet Buzz's charming wife, Sarah.

Mrs. Olson's table was beautifully set for her dinner. A cluster of red roses from her garden graced the white linen tablecloth set for twelve diners. Mrs. Olson showed off her talents as a sophisticated hostess, using her best silverware and English Spode bone china, designed with floral patterns of rose, yellow and green.

The guests soon began exchanging bits of news and gossip with one another. "Did you know Mrs. Smith had to be rushed over to a Wayzata doctor's office for treatment of an ulcer?"..."How's your daughter doing with the new baby?"..."Our dogs took off today and have not returned." So went the chitchat early in the evening.

Soon Mrs. Olson invited the guests to be seated around the table. After everyone was seated and they had said grace, she nodded toward Macie. "I've invited all of you to this little dinner to introduce you to our guest for the summer, Macie Stewart. I thought that she would benefit from meeting you all to help her feel at home around here. So, let's just go around the table and introduce ourselves. Ella, could you please start us off?"

"Surely. I'm Ella Severson. I'm a teacher and I'm the clerk for the Episcopal church."

Mrs. Olson chimed in at this point. "Ella is the most dedicated church clerk you'll ever meet. She's also humble. The congregation has given her the title 'clerk for life'.[12] She probably has more influence in our community than all the town's ministers combined."

Ella merely smiled.

The gentleman to her right spoke next. "I'm Ella's husband, George. I'm a carpenter. We have two sons, both of whom are married and have moved to Wayzata on the opposite end of the lake. We have no grandchildren yet – although we're watching closely for them." With that, he smiled broadly.

Buzz was next. "You all know me and my wife, Sarah. I met Macie yesterday when she arrived with Mr. Jerome at the St. Louis Hotel. I think she's pretty impressed with our lake."

"Ed?" Mrs. Olson prompted the sheriff to go next.

"Sorry," he replied. "I'm Ed Herman and this here's my wife, Dorothy. We don't have any children. I'm the Excelsior sheriff." The Hermans turned to their right indicating the next woman's turn to speak.

"Hello, I'm Meranda Delaquila. I just met my new friend, Macie, this morning and the Olsons were nice enough to include me here tonight. I'm originally from New Orleans but I've been living for most of my adult life in St. Paul. I've never married. I own some properties in St. Paul but, I must say, I love this relaxed and scenic little town. It's a great place to vacation away from the big city."

Macie spoke next. "Hello, I'm Macie Stewart. I'm in town this summer working as a bookkeeper for Mr. Will Jerome in the St. Louis

Hotel. I just finished my schooling but I'm thinking that I may return to school again in the near future to become an attorney."

"I don't think it's possible for women to become attorneys, is it?" Mr. Olson asked.

"Mr. Jerome has encouraged me to think about studying the law. He believes that I could succeed in that field," Macie replied.

Meranda jumped in immediately. "I think women are just as capable of things as men are. They may not be as physically strong, but with appropriate education, I think women can do just about anything that they set their minds to. I believe that things will be very different in the future."

After a brief pause as startled expressions started to wane, the next gentleman took the floor. "Welcome to Excelsior, Macie. We hope that you have a great summer in our town. I'm Babbs Iger[13] and this is my wife, Augusta. We have three young children at home, two boys and a girl. I'm the local blacksmith."

"Oh, there's more that must be said about Babbs," Mrs. Olson interjected. "Babbs has a very famous client! Macie, perhaps you've heard of Dan Patch, the record-setting harness racehorse? Babbs works on that horse."

"Yes, the stable for the horse is located just south of the Minnesota River," Mr. Olson added. "Babbs has been hired by Marion Savage, the horse's owner, to keep the horse in ideal horseshoes. That horse is unbeatable."

"Golly!" Macie replied.

"And there is more that we must add about Babbs!" Mrs. Olson continued. "He's known far and wide for his fabulous dill pickles. He has honored us by contributing some of his famous pickles for our dinner tonight. And, speaking of dinner, thank you all for introducing yourselves but it's time to eat. I'll fetch the walleye."

Town Talk

Later in the evening, the guests were finishing their delicious fried walleye dinner when a latecomer arrived. The Olsons were pleased to welcome him with Mr. Olson making his introduction. "Macie and Meranda, this is our architect friend, Keith Duggan. He's designed a lot of the buildings in our town and he is currently working on Big Island Park."

Macie felt a certain spark as she beheld Keith. She fought off the urge to blush. She thought him an extremely attractive fellow, tall and lanky with somewhat reddish hair, and guessed he was probably in his early to mid-30s. She also admired the aura of confidence he exuded.

"Keith, please have a seat at the table and I'll fix you a plate. We can't have you going hungry." Mrs. Olson soon returned from the kitchen with a heaping plate which she set in front of Keith.

"Thank you very much, Mrs. Olson. That's so nice of you. Sorry that I'm so late, but I couldn't break away from a meeting with a client that went very long."

"Wow! He's also very polite!" Macie thought.

The topic of conversation at the table soon turned to items in the local news.

"There's been a lot happening in town of late," Mrs. Olson noted, directing her comments toward Macie. "Unfortunately, some of that news is not good. Sheriff, could you please give us an update on some of the things that have been keeping you so busy?"

"Of course," the sheriff replied. "The routine stuff alone has kept me very busy. And, as you're all aware, despite the summer rains, there have been an unusual number of fires in the area."

"What fires are you currently investigating, Sheriff?" Mrs. Olson asked.

"There was the fire that destroyed the Christian college last week. There was the one two weeks ago that was caught in time at the General Store. There was the fire behind the bank before that — another one that was caught before it could do much damage. All those fires seemed suspicious since they all appeared to have started outside the buildings."

"It's scary to think that we may have an arsonist in town," Mr. Iger noted.

"It is, indeed," his wife replied. "Are we dealing with a pyromaniac?"

"You know, there's something that links all of the fires you just mentioned, Sheriff," Buzz observed.

"There is?" the sheriff replied with a furled brow.

"All those fires are tied to buildings associated with members of our town council," Buzz continued. "Bob Meier, the bank president; Don Greene, owner of the General Store; Dave Walters, the president of the college."

"Hmmm...I hadn't thought of that. Great observation, Buzz. Does someone have a grudge against our council?"

"There are always people who disagree with something or other that the council does. It's impossible to please everyone," Buzz said.

"But to think someone's that angry and crazy..." Mrs. Iger noted, shaking her head.

"Unfortunately, I've not been able to make much progress in figuring out what caused the fires. I wish that I could hire a deputy to help with all this."

"Thank you, Sheriff. We know that you're doing your best to keep us safe," Mrs. Olson said.

A moment of silence prevailed as the mood in the room had become somber. Mrs. Iger was not yet done with the topic. "Ella, we heard the school bells last night but apparently there was no fire. Do you know anything on that?"

"Yes, it was a prank. A couple of kids up to no good," Ella replied.[14]

"That's awful!" Mrs. Iger responded.

Mrs. Olson changed the focus. "Keith, what's the latest on the Big Island park decision? Have you heard anything about how Wayzata is reacting to the potential park? Are they jealous?"

"I bet they're all upset over there what with Twin City Rapid Transit investing so much in our town," Mr. Iger suggested.

"They don't care as long as they've got J.J. Hill developing lakefront acreage near their property limits," quipped Mr. Olson.

Keith then took the floor. "As for Big Island Park, as most of you know from ongoing news reports, it's going to be original and very big on sixty-five acres of land. It will be a huge contributor to our town's economy, attracting thousands of people. However, in town council meetings, it's still pretty contentious. The mayor and key town leaders appear to support the park but there are several townspeople who continually voice their strong opposition. They worry that proceeding with the park will start a moral deterioration in our town, especially around drinking. They favor our current law against alcohol and fear what happened in White Bear Lake with its park: bringing some unsavory people to town and increasing public drunkenness. They think that drinking will also lead to increased crime."

Meranda took the floor. "Those teetotalers are being ridiculous! The park would be great for this town. Their fears about alcohol abuse are way overblown. Your town could use some livening up."

The frowns and silence made it clear that not everyone at the table shared Meranda's views.

Keith finally broke the icy silence. "There's a key town council meeting tomorrow that could well determine the park's fate. I think that Will Jerome throwing his support behind the park will really make a difference." A chorus of little, muffled comments amongst the dinner guests followed his announcement.

The Igers stood up and announced that they needed to be going. Others then joined them with choruses of "thanks" being shared with the Olsons for their welcoming hospitality.

To Macie's delight, Keith made his way over to her and extended his hand to welcome her to town. "You'll like the folks here, Macie. This is a wonderful town. If you'd be interested, I'd be happy to show you around a bit."

Macie, feeling uncharacteristically shy, did manage to reply. "That sounds wonderful."

"Will you be at the council meeting tomorrow?"

"Yes, I'll be there with Mr. Jerome."

"Wonderful! I'll look for you there." Keith then left the boarding house.

Macie wondered if she'd be able to sleep tonight.

Decisions

    This was an important event at town hall. The fate of the proposed Big Island Park lay in the hands of the Excelsior town council.

    Attending the meeting were the mayor, Don Greene, owner of the general store, and council members Bob Meier, president of the bank; Dan Stucki, owner of the sawmill; Dave Walters, the college president; and Glenn Pusch, the barber. Other special guests invited for this meeting included Sheriff Herman; Will Jerome; Vegas Thorpe, a private attorney; architect Keith Duggan; and Thomas Louden[15], founder of the Twin City Rapid Transit and the primary sponsor of the park. Pastor Winfield of the Episcopal church was there along with Ella Severson. Covering the event for the *Excelsior Journal* was Buzz. Macie was also present to take notes. A dozen or so townspeople had also squeezed into the room to observe the proceedings with dozens more listening outside the door.

The mayor called the special meeting to order. "I think we have three key items on our agenda, all relating to the proposed Big Island Park. First are the concerns that have been raised about the park's financing. Second, we need to talk about the expressed opposition to the park by some of our key townspeople. Then, if we can reach resolution in those areas, we can make a final vote on the park. Does anyone have any thoughts on that agenda or additional items to add?"

The mayor's question was greeted with silence. "Okay. I'd like to call on Mr. Thorpe, city attorney, to briefly review the financing for this project." Thorpe, a bookish-looking man with strong eyeglasses, replied: "Certainly. The bulk of the park's financing is provided by the

Twin Cities Rapid Transit Company represented here today by its founder, Mr. Thomas Louden. His company is very sound financially as their transit system has expanded throughout the Twin Cities. TCRT stock has increased from about $10 a few years ago to about $100 as of late. They already own a similar park over in St. Paul. That park, Wildwood, has proved to be extremely profitable. It has exceeded expectations and there is confidence that the Big Island park will be equally successful. Mr. Jerome, who is already well known within this community, has recently agreed to participate in the funding of the park as a minority partner. The park will be very well capitalized."

"I agree with Mr. Thorpe's summary on the project," Will Jerome added. "Our guest today, Thomas Louden of the TCRT, is a visionary and successful business leader. He and I and our organizations have reviewed all aspects of this project. Mr. Louden and I are both very excited about it and we have no reservations about the project funding. We think our plans for the park will provide a place for the public to thoroughly enjoy themselves."

"Does anyone have further questions for Mr. Jerome, Mr. Louden, or Mr. Thorpe?"

"No, that helps me feel more comfortable," Dave Walters said. Other council members seemed to be nodding their approval.

"I've got a question for Mr. Duggan," councilmember Stucki proposed. "Is the financing adequate given your projections for the project cost?"

"Yes, it is," Keith replied. "Actually, there's even some cushion."

The mayor then continued: "All right, let's move on to our second agenda item. How do we help our town to become more comfortable with this park?"

"Most of their resistance seems to be around alcohol, right?" Bob Meier inquired.

"That would seem to be the case," Vegas Thorpe replied.

"They don't want to see people staggering around 'How came you so'." Sheriff Herman added from his seat in the gallery.

"How came you so?[16]" inquired Mayor Greene.

"Sorry. Drunk," the sheriff clarified.

"So, any ideas folks?" the mayor inquired. "Most people in our town are clearly in favor of our laws against alcohol."

Pastor Winfield stood up and spoke, as he sensed that this was Ella Severson's entrée. "Mr. Mayor and members of the council, I would like to let Ella Severson speak to that topic as I don't think there is anyone in our town who is more connected to the entire Excelsior religious community than she is. Ella."

Ella stood up, a Bible in hand, and began: "Galatians chapter 5 tells us that the acts of the sinful nature are obvious. Drunkenness is the first act mentioned. The Bible then continues: 'I warn you, as I did before, that those who live like this will not inherit the kingdom of God.'" She paused briefly to let her point sink in. "Hopefully we agree that the Bible is pretty clear." Ella then retook her seat.

"Yes, we're not going to change our laws around alcohol for the sake of this park. Thoughts on how to address this concern?" the mayor prompted.

"I think there's an obvious solution to this problem," Mr. Louden began. "The property that we, the TCRT, have acquired used to contain a campground that became known as a groggery or beer garden. We own the property now. The groggery is gone, and we can set our own rules. We don't want drunkenness within our transit system any more than you want it within your community. Therefore, we'll abide by your city laws enforcing prohibition within our park. While alcohol is allowed at Wildwood over in St. Paul and it has created some minor problems, there's clearly room for different types of parks. The Big Island park will be promoted as a family-friendly destination."

"That sounds like the perfect solution to me," the mayor replied. "Our town can benefit from the increased tourism and commerce without altering our stance on alcohol. Does anyone want further discussion on this topic?"

A hand went up in the back of the room from a citizen. "Will the park lead to an increase in our taxes?"

"No, it will not. The park is being totally financed privately," the mayor replied.

Another hand went up. "Who's going to provide security at the park?"

Tom Louden took this question. "We will be employing several security personnel on the park staff."

"Any other questions?" the mayor asked. After a pause and hearing no further discussion, the mayor continued. "I move that we vote to approve the plans for Big Island park."

"I second the motion," added Bob Meier.

The mayor continued: "All in favor say 'aye'."

Five voices sounded in unison.

"All opposed say 'nay'." Silence was the response.

A small commotion broke out in the back of the room. "We don't want this park!" shouted one man. Another shouted, "Get rid of this council! Satan is at work within them! Alcohol will be a problem again!"

"Order!" shouted the mayor banging his gavel on the desk. The commotion ceased. "The park is approved! I'm sorry that there are still a few citizens who oppose the park. We were elected to represent the best interests of the overall community. Mr. Louden, Mr. Jerome, set to building your park! Mr. Greenfield, I trust that you will print a little summary article in the next edition of the paper?"

"Yes, we definitely will. Front page news!" Buzz replied. "Could I get a photograph for this important article?"[17]

"Sure, Mr. Greenfield," the mayor responded.

"It'll take me just a couple of minutes to get set up," Buzz noted, starting to move his equipment into position. Once ready, he continued: "I'm going to take this photo using some new technology. I've done some practice on my own. I've placed some special powder on this little platform." He held the platform aloft in front of the council members seated at their table. "When I activate the shutter on my camera, the powder will ignite, and you will hear a small explosion that will light up the room for my photo. Ready?"

"All right, Mr. Greenfield," replied the mayor.

Buzz was right as the resulting bright light and explosion was somewhat startling despite the warning.

"Thank you all," Buzz said, obviously pleased at capturing his first indoor photo.

"I move that we adjourn the meeting," Mayor Greene continued.

"I second that," Bob Meier replied.

"Any objections? No? The meeting is adjourned. Thank you all."

Keith

Following the town council meeting, Keith caught up with Macie. "Macie, do you have time for a little walk with me?"

Macie turned, smiling as she heard his voice. "Keith, I knew that was your voice right away. Do you have some nice spots to show me around here?" she asked.

"Well... sure," replied Keith. "Let's head this way," Keith pointed toward a church a short distance ahead. "First the oldest church in town, I love its architecture. You'll see why. And it's right on the way to the beach down by the Commons."

Macie smiled shyly as they began their walk. Keith reached for her hand. She tensed instinctively for a second at the surprise. He gave no clue that he detected her reaction, his grasp calming and soothing. She relaxed. They continued in silence for a bit and then began to swing their arms playfully back and forth. She had never really had a boyfriend before and she felt the way her heart was beating, that maybe Keith could be it.

He stopped suddenly in front of Trinity Episcopal Church. He then dropped her hand and began gesturing to explain why he admired it so much. "See, Macie, it's like a small English church in its proportions. See how it's made? Look at the roof, a high gable for its time. And the whole structure, built of native materials, like lakeshore stone and local timbers. It has a special form that I admire."

This was the first woman he had ever talked to about architecture and there was something about young Macie that lit a spark in him.

"Oh Keith, you know so much! I would like to go in it sometime." As she spoke, she could not help noticing how attractive he looked, tall, tailored yet casual, wearing a different style jacket than Mr. Jerome's. "He just looks like an architect is supposed to look in stature and bearing," she said to herself, "and he has confidence in what he's doing."

They resumed their walk as Macie continued: "And please tell me more about your plans for Big Island Park."

"Sure! It will occupy about half of the northern shore of the island. It will have facilities for picnicking, concerts, rides and all kinds of entertainment. But rather than describe it here, I think it would be better if I describe it while actually out on the island. I'd like to take you there to show you the park property, but I'd be afraid for you. There have been so many drownings."

"That would be delightful, and you'd have nothing to worry about. I'm a very strong swimmer."

"All right, we have a plan!"

The young couple, holding hands again as they walked, soon approached a broad sandy beach where children were playing in the water as their watchful mothers looked on.

"How 'bout a little wading, Macie?" gestured Keith, taking off his shoes and rolling up his trousers a little.

"What fun!" shouted Macie, following his example, just slightly lifting her dress hem in a maidenly way.

After wading in the shallow water for a bit, Keith returned to the shore and spread out the blanket he'd been carrying for them. They sat down together while gazing out at the beautiful lake. "So, who is Macie Stewart? Please don't keep me in suspense." asked Keith.

Macie shrugged, shaking her blonde head as though she was about to tell him something important. "I'm an orphan, Keith."

She then proceeded to tell him about the death of her parents in the fire, her adoption by the Stewarts, her delightful relationship with her stepmother and her stormy relationship with her stepfather. "So, I was lucky to get this job with Mr. Jerome. He has treated me like family. While I don't have a close relationship with my stepfather, I must give him some credit as I know he played a role in helping me to get this job."

Keith felt somewhat mystified by her life compared to his. "Guess I was lucky, Macie. I'm part of a normal, southern Minnesota farming family. My father did well and all four of us were able to attend college. I got my architecture degree at the University of Minnesota. It's a pretty mundane story."

"Oh, but I've heard that architecture can be a very exciting profession. Do you have big projects lined up after Big Island Park?"

Keith, smiling replied. "Well I don't think I can get to be another LeRoy Buffington, who did so much fine work in Minneapolis and at our lake, designing hotels, churches, art galleries and homes. But I'd like to design really good homes like the one Mr. Jerome has now over on the west shore. He calls it 'North home' or 'Northome.' "

"Yes, he's proud of that home too."

Keith paused then continued. "I hope you really like being here in Minnesota with us. We want you to feel at home." Turning closer to her and whispering softly into her ear, "Especially me!" giving her a quick kiss on the cheek.

It had been a wonderful day for Macie as Keith left her at the Olson's door. Her head was whirling with happiness, her skin was tingling as she threw off her petticoat and danced around her room. "Maybe I'm in love," she thought. "Whatever it is, I know I'm crazy about him."

Confidantes

Having coffee the next morning with Mrs. Olson, Macie learned about some of the recent gossip. Apparently, some of the church ladies are disturbed about Meranda's unconventional wardrobe and wonder why she looks so out of place. The head of the Episcopal women's circle has stated that she is personally going to befriend her and get her involved in the church. Mrs. Severson has mentioned that "Maybe she can sing." Someone else thought that perhaps Meranda could pour tea for their receptions. Others piped up with other ways to convince Meranda to join their group and maybe do some quilting together.

Hearing this, Macie announced: "Well, I like Meranda. I feel a real connection with her. I'm going to call on her this morning."

Macie found Meranda at home in her apartment.

"Hello, honey. You are looking so pretty. Where are you off to today?" Meranda asked.

Macie blurted, "I just need your advice. I think I'm falling in love and I don't know how to act or what to do about it. Have any tips for me?"

With a big grin, Meranda continued, "Come on in and make yourself comfortable," pointing at the two cozy chairs. "I just made a pot of coffee. Care for a cup?"

"Yes, please."

Meranda began while getting the coffee. "If this is your first beau, go easy. Don't let him know how you feel just yet. There is a lot of timing when it comes to romance."

"What d'ya mean, 'timing'?" Macie asks.

"Has he kissed you yet, honey?"

"Yes – on the cheek. We've held hands. And I felt like I was going to the moon," beamed Macie, blushing. "Keith is just divine, I think."

"Oh, you mean the architect Keith? My oh my! What a handsome fellow! Now you've got to play this right," says Meranda.

"How so?" Macie reminded her that she doesn't have a home to invite him to.

Meranda responded "How 'bout arranging to see Keith somewhere outdoors -- like on a nice moonlit night? Maybe you could take one of those moonlight cruises aboard the St. Louis boat that I've heard about."

"That's a wonderful idea," Macie replied.

"Here's another suggestion for you. Do you journal in a diary?"

"No, never have."

"I've been journaling for years. I keep my diary handy," she said, pointing to an open book on her table, "although I haven't been writing much this summer. I have this running conversation with myself. I think it's a useful tool for increasing self-understanding. You might start journaling to keep memories alive about your exciting new relationship and to explore your inner thoughts about it."

"That's a good idea, too." Macie paused, drank some coffee, then continued, although her expression had changed to one that seemed somber. "On another topic, the other day, you mentioned a desire to see the photos of my parents. I brought 'em along today." She opened an envelope. "This is the only photo that I have of me with my parents," Macie said, handing her two photos.

Meranda saw a lovely young couple standing in front of what appeared to be their farmhouse. They were both looking at the beautiful baby in the arms of the mother. Meranda reached out to place her arm around Macie. "I'm very sorry, Macie." Shifting to the second photo, Meranda exclaimed,

"Wow! Tell me about this one of your father."

"That's him holding his prized possession. It's a gold nugget that he inherited from his brother. According to my grandmother, it's one of the largest nuggets ever found in Montana."

The photo showed her father from the waist up, holding a very large nugget in what appeared to be a protective container.

"It's huge!" Meranda exclaimed. "And it's kind of an unusual shape. It almost looks like a fish."

"Apparently, they called it 'the whale' for exactly that reason. My grandmother tells me that his nugget disappeared in the house fire. That's about all the story I can recall. These photos remind me that I'm going to have to ask my grandmother again about my parents."

"Thanks for sharing your photos with me, Macie. I'm very touched," handing the photos back to Macie then hugging her with both arms this time.

"Oh, Meranda. Thank you. Thank you for the coffee and your relationship advice. Most importantly, thank you for your friendship. But now I need to be off to work." Macie arose and headed for the door. "See ya soon."

On her way to the office, she ran into Buzz again. "Macie", he shouted. "Big news: There's been a knifing at the St. Louis Hotel! I'm on my way to see about it. Maybe the sheriff is over there now."

"That's terrible, Buzz! Who would think such a thing could happen way out here in Excelsior, and at Mr. Jerome's hotel too," cried Macie. "I'm on my way to the hotel too. We've got to be careful."

Progress

A few hours later, Buzz found Macie in her little office. "Apparently, a member of Mr. Jerome's staff spotted someone setting fire to a tool shed on the far side of the hotel property. When that staff member yelled out to stop the arsonist, someone emerged from the bushes behind him and stabbed him. The two arsonists then took off through the woods to the east. Fortunately, the knife just grazed him and he is expected to be fine."

"Wow!" Macie replied.

"Unfortunately, the building and all of the gardening equipment within was a total loss. I've got to get to the office to write up this story but I wanted to give you an update. The plague of the arsonists continues. Please be careful, Macie."

"Thanks, Buzz. That's certainly a troubling piece of news. But thank goodness you're keeping our community informed. Have a good day," Macie wished him as he headed back to town.

Macie returned her attention to the dwindling piles of documents still awaiting sorting and filing. Review of all the documents caused several key questions to be raised in her mind. The most significant related to a steady stream of invoices from the Vegas Thorpe law firm. The hotel was clearly spending a significant sum of money for legal guidance. She decided to consult with the hotel manager.

He was in his office when she arrived. "Mr. Adams, I've made a lot of progress on filing of the documents."

"So I've noticed!" he replied. "Thanks for your efforts. I trust that you have another question for me."

"I do. I'm curious about all of the payments to the law firm of Vegas Thorpe."

"I can help with that. The hotel has engaged the services of his firm since he came to Excelsior with Mr. Jerome about fifteen years ago. A few years later he launched his own firm. He represents our hotel in a variety of legal matters. Unfortunately, his work for us in handling of insurance claims has become increasingly important. Most of those claims focused around property damage from fire – like the one we suffered again today. Another terrible loss! Someone could have been killed!"

"Yes, that's really scary!"

"We finally have some evidence that arsonists are behind at least some of these fires. We've got to catch them."

"Yes. As for Vegas Thorpe, it's good that you have legal representation, but those services are a significant drain on the resources of the hotel."

"I can't disagree with you on that," he replied. "Anything else that I can help you with today?"

"No but I'll undoubtedly have more questions for you in the days to come. Thank you."

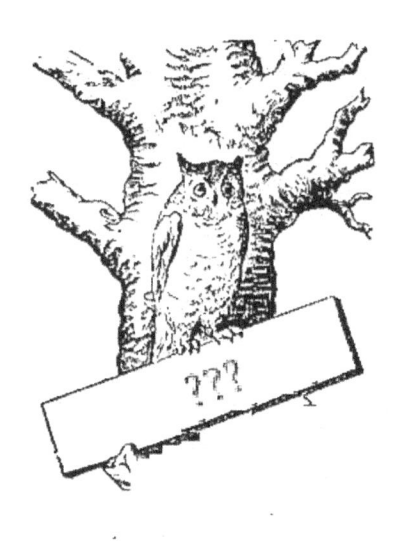

Tea

Back at the boarding house, Mrs. Olson entered the room and welcomed Macie asking if she had made any new friends.

Macie shrugged. "Well, I've really become good friends with Meranda. I know that some folks in town don't seem to approve of her. But I like her. She's refreshingly different and we seem to have a lot to gab about."

Mrs. Olson was surprised at Macie's new friend. "Well you don't really have much in common, do you?"

"Even though we're quite different in age, there's mutual respect between us, and we really enjoy each other's company. We're also talking about ways to help each other. Meranda's helping me with my new relationship with Keith. And, she's trying to deal with some things from her past that she's not very proud of --although she hasn't really gone into much detail about those things. She has told me that I'm a good listener."

"Maybe she thought a big change in setting would help and she came here to our little town on the lake to make some progress in her life."

"Yes, I think Mrs. Severson and other ladies from the church are trying hard to influence her," Macie said smiling, "but I don't think Meranda is the churchy type."

Mrs. Olson laughed at Macie's reaction. "I admit. I don't see her going to services at all. But she does seem to like cooking, I mean like fixing cookies and little tarts and other sweets. She's already done that once for Mrs. Peterson's funeral the other day. Maybe she'd be willing to become more active in the church if her commitment started with just cooking."

"I think there is a church ladies' tea tomorrow morning. Perhaps I could encourage Meranda to take part in it with me."

"Good idea."

After making a few arrangements, Macie succeeded in bringing Meranda to the Episcopal church and the Ladies Guild's monthly tea. Meranda arrived dressed appropriately for the occasion, wearing a soft brown print calico dress topped with a large feathered hat to match her brown eyes. To the delight of the other ladies, she was carrying a plate of freshly baked sugar cookies.

Several women including the wife of the mayor joined their table.

"We're so pleased that you could join us today, Meranda," said Mrs. Severson, chair of the women's group. After some typical socializing, Mrs. Severson nodded to Meranda. "You said you come from St Paul. We get very little news from the capital city here in Excelsior. Could you fill us in a bit?"

"Surely," Meranda began. "Generally, it's a nice city to live in. But it's growing very rapidly – a bit too rapidly, in my opinion."

"What's the effect of the population growth?" another woman asked.

"Unfortunately," Meranda replied, "St. Paul seems to be attracting an increasing number of unsavory people. Crime is a growing problem. I've been touched by it directly."

"Oh, oh" said Mrs. Severson, looking horrified. "I hope that it was nothing serious."

"Unfortunately, it was," Meranda replied.

"We're here to support you, if you'd care to share more," Mrs. Severson replied.

"All right. One night, an acquaintance of mine knocked on my door. When I opened the door, I could tell immediately that he was drunk. He forced his way in." Her audience seemed to draw a collective breath.

Another woman asked, "Meranda, weren't you afraid?"

Meranda smiled, "At first I was because he pushed me against the wall yelling that he wanted another drink. But I had my wits about me. I just calmly told him to follow me to the kitchen."

"It's hard to believe that you could be calm in that situation. I sure couldn't," Mrs. Severson added.

The group responded nearly in unison by shaking their heads.

"He let go of me and followed. I grabbed my rolling pin and threatened to bash him if he didn't leave. He tried to grab the rolling pin, but he didn't move very well in his drunken state. I gave him a good shot to the body. He went reeling, got up, then staggered out of my house."

"Wow! Good for you! You were also very lucky. That could have turned out very differently," another woman replied.

The group was shocked but thanked Meranda for sharing. One member commented, "It's a good thing we have laws here in Excelsior preventing people from using liquor." Another lady said, "Meranda, we feel that Jesus would not want us to be drinking. Don't you agree?"

"I'm not sure about that. I have always enjoyed wine and even an occasional cocktail. And I have not yet really made up my mind about Jesus. I appreciate your efforts to help me with my doubts but I'm not there yet."

"If it's all right with you, we will continue to pray for you, Meranda."

"That's fine. I appreciate your patience with me and your companionship."

After the desserts were served, Macie accompanied Meranda back to her apartment. While walking, they talked about the meeting. After leaving Meranda, Macie caught the next launch to the hotel. As she walked into her office, she noticed an envelope with her name on it that was prominently placed on her desk. She opened it immediately and was delighted by its contents: An invitation to the Grand Ball! She had heard rumblings about the upcoming event and how it would now also celebrate the council approval for the Big Island Park. It was guaranteed to be a festive event attracting many important people. She felt very fortunate to be included at the last minute.

    She found it hard to concentrate on her work during the rest of that day with her thoughts continually returning to the ball. After an hour or two, she finally decided that further efforts with her work for the moment were futile. Instead it was time to go off and see about a new dress, a gown for the ball. Macie's face brightened at the thought.

Maybe Mrs. O. could help her with that.

The Grand Ball

YOU ARE INVITED TO THE GRAND BALL AT THE ST. LOUIS HOTEL Saturday, July 22, 1899 at 9 p.m.

Macie reread the invitation to celebrate approval of the park, giddy with happiness. She knew that Mr. Jerome and his committee had been planning this for weeks. The event would take place in the second-floor ballroom of the hotel where it had been scrubbed and draped and polished for the occasion. Special chairs ringed the dance floor plus assorted tables and chairs were positioned at one end. Electric lights, replacing the old gas lamps, lit up the area and beautiful bouquets of fresh flowers decorated the tables. Already set was the stage for the band specially chosen by Will Jerome himself, who liked certain kinds of music for dancing such as waltzes and polkas. His luxurious hotel was ready to show itself off to many out-of-town guests who were already staying there and to the many local invitees. Excitement was in the air!

Meanwhile, Mrs. O. was pinning final touches to the ballgown she had selected for Macie. It was an elegant creation of soft blue silk and taffeta over layers of petticoats that made the skirt fill out and swing.

"Stand still, Macie," ordered Mrs. O. sternly. "This is your final fitting."

Macie obeyed until Mrs. O. had finished then began twirling around the room. "Oh Mrs. O., you are a dear to tailor this for me. It's the prettiest dress I've ever had!" she exclaimed.

Promptly at 8:45 that evening, Macie and Keith joined a host of other friends boarding a crowded ferry boat to take them across the bay to Deephaven and the hotel. Every man was dressed to the nines in starched white shirts and bow ties. Even Buzz, out of his boating clothes for once, wore a new tie and a nice coat.

Once ashore at the hotel, Macie took a good look around just to gaze at the fashions the women were wearing. Mrs. Severson was wearing a stiff-looking gold-colored gown. The wife of bank president Bob Meier came in a ruffled white blouse with a pink piqué flared skirt and Meranda sported a red and white silk gown with little sparkles on the fabric. For this occasion, she had pinned up her dark brown hair with a rhinestone hair comb. In general, all the ladies present were attired in attractive ball gowns that reached the floor and were perfect for the big occasion.

Later in the evening, when the dancing was in full swing, Macie and Keith sat out a song to catch their breath. After watching the gentle rise and fall of the waltzing dancers in time with the music, Macie shared an observation with Keith. "Everyone is just so happy tonight! Even that attorney is finally smiling," she noted, nodding in the direction of normally staid Vegas Thorpe, dancing enthusiastically with Meranda. "What a wonderful event! And what incredible timing for this event after the park has finally been approved."

Mr. Jerome and his lovely, much-admired wife commanded the floor as they waltzed effortlessly and gracefully around the room. Buzz, on the other hand, stumbled occasionally while trying to lead his wife. Despite the dancing challenges, his radiant smile persisted.

Their energy renewed, Keith and Macie soon returned to the dance floor.

Buzz, who had brought his camera along for this glamorous event, left the dance floor, preparing to take some photos. He returned to the ball and took a few shots of key couples: Mr. and Mrs. Jerome, the mayors of Excelsior and Wayzata and their wives, a few business and church leaders from Excelsior, plus several dignitaries from Minneapolis including Thomas Louden of the TCRT and his wife and several other prominent couples. Buzz then put away his work for the evening. To Macie and Keith, he said: "You two were having more fun than anyone else."

It was the end of a wonderful, exciting evening for Macie. "Oh, Keith, this was my first ever ball. I loved every minute of it - especially because I was with you."

Big Island

Keith approached Macie late the following Friday as she was leaving Mr. Jerome's office.

"Macie, are you free tomorrow? I've thought of a place where I'd like to take you." He admitted that it would be an adventure.

"An adventure?" said Macie, her face already animated. "Sounds exciting. Yes, I'd certainly love to join you in your mysterious adventure."

"You have to come prepared, because we're going out in my canoe to Big Island," said Keith.

"But I've never been in a canoe. You mean the boats like the Indians used to have? What do I wear? You'll have to teach me," replied Macie, arching her eyebrows.

"I'll show you how to paddle the canoe. It's easy. You'll need to wear something to cover you up for walking in brush, and maybe over your bathing dress in case the lake is rough. Is that okay with you?" asked Keith.

"Sure." Macie wasn't very sure at all about this, but trusted Keith to carry it out.

The next day, a hot but beautiful Saturday morning, they took off. Keith had placed Macie in the bow since most of the control and steering of the canoe is up to the person in the stern. He thought she looked great up there in her white blouse and print skirt. It was a slow start in the calm waters of the bay, as Macie gradually learned how to use the paddle while maintaining her balance in the boat. She was not exactly nervous but felt a bit tentative as she began, then grinned broadly as the canoe responded. With each stroke, her confidence increased.

Soon they had reached the main waters of the big lake where Keith urged her to paddle harder. She responded as directed and Keith was stunned to see the canoe suddenly surge forward. She could see Big Island way ahead and grimaced internally at the effort required to reach it. Keith coaxed her to relax a bit as he could tell that her new pace would not be sustainable.

"You're doing very well, Macie! It won't take us too long to get there," said Keith calmly. A gentle wind from the south helped propel their canoe closer and closer to the island. After about 30 minutes of paddling, they were finally approaching the sandy shore. Suddenly, Macie cried out: "Keith! A rock!" She immediately reached out ahead with her paddle trying to push the front of the canoe away from the large rock hidden just below the surface. The sudden shift in weight overturned the canoe, launching both of them into the water. In an instant, as she surfaced, Macie felt Keith's strong arms enveloping her and carrying her toward the shore.

Keith, overcome by her lovely young body, her clothes clinging to her bosom, passionately embraced her, whispering, "Macie, I love you, love you, you are my darling, lovely one. "

Macie returned his heartfelt kisses, with a tenderness she had never felt before, repeating "I love you too, Keith."

They sat down on shore, leisurely snuggling. The intense rays of the sun eventually brought them back to reality. Macie tore off her wet clothing, revealing her long bathing dress underneath and shouted, "Let's go for a swim, Keith," starting to wade back into the lake. He quickly hung up her clothing to dry on the bushes then plunged in after her. They embraced again when reaching the deep water, each loving the feel of the other's body. Then, gradually feeling the chill, they slowly swam back to shore. Keith shouted, "Let's lie down on my blanket to dry off in the sun a bit before I show you around here."

Huddled on top of the blanket and basking in the warm sunshine, they laughed like two kids cast adrift on an island ala Robinson Crusoe. They nibbled on the fruit and cheese that Keith had brought in a picnic basket. After a while, Keith jumped into his clothing, tied down the canoe and helped Macie find her clothes, now dry enough thanks to the sun and wind. When she was ready, he grabbed her hand and led her off to a large dock nearby. "This, my love, is where the Amusement Park begins. Watch and I'll explain what I have designed."

With sweeping gestures, Keith explained, "This will be the main picnic grounds, where people can sit in the shade of these big trees, elms and oaks, and we'll have some tables and chairs for them too." Then, getting more excited, the architect pointed north explaining "This will be a paved sidewalk leading to a great tower. Very high, like a water tower. Only this will be a Light Tower, filled with so many electric lights it will light up this whole area and people will be able to see it for miles around on the lake."

"My! Will there be other buildings too, Keith?" asked Macie, listening breathlessly.

"Oh, yes indeed, Macie." Pointing as he narrated, "We'll have a food hall over there along the shore and a music casino back in that area. I've designed all the buildings using the Spanish Mission style of architecture: white stucco with red tile roofs. Follow me. Just like the famous architect, Leroy Buffington, I've tried to give the island a 'City Beautiful'[18] look."

Keith led Macie through the brush along the shore until they arrived at the base of a gentle hill.

"There will be a large amphitheater carved into the back of this hillside. And, for fun, there will be a rollercoaster and other rides on the far side of the island over that way. Imagine that: a rollercoaster on Big Island!"

"I've heard that Twin City Rapid Transit has one operating over on Wildwood, St Paul," said Macie.

"Yes, TCRT also has big hopes for this park, Macie. And so do I. We're starting this week. We did the dock first so the big ferries can bring in all the building materials."

With the light dwindling, the two clasped hands and returned to the canoe. By now the southerly wind had subsided so they could easily paddle home, looking a bit bedraggled but very happy.

Nighttime

Meranda awoke with a start as something touched her throat. She opened her eyes to sense a face within inches of hers. The impending scream was squelched when cloth was stuffed into her mouth. The darkness prevented her from seeing the intruder.

"Careful, bitch! I'd hate to have this knife slip and slit your throat open. Don't move!"

She realized that resistance was futile as he climbed astride her, pinning her arms to the bed beneath his knees.

"It's payback time!" he muttered quietly. "Cooperate and you just might survive our little session together." She felt something being tied to her left wrist. Then her right wrist was tied. With her body immobilized by the weight of his body, she then felt him reach under the covers for her right ankle. Something was tied to it. He then repeated the process with her left ankle.

With her body completely secured on the bed, he arose. He lit a match and then lit the lantern on the table. She gasped internally. Her St. Paul attacker!

"First, we find some of the money that you owe me." He pulled open the top drawer from the chest, rifling through the contents, flipping some of the garments to the floor. "I know it's here somewhere." He repeated the process with the second and third drawers. Finding nothing but clothes, he moved to the closet. He quickly slid each garment between his hands from top to bottom. Finding nothing, he turned his attention to the boxes on the closet shelf. He dumped the contents one by one onto the floor, revealing more items of clothing.

"I'm getting a bit tired of this," he growled under his breath. "Let's get you ready for our little play session together." He returned to the bed, grabbed the top of her nightgown and pulled, ripping it the length of her body. "There! Nice!" he gloated, examining the length of her exposed body. "You're ready now. I'll look a bit further now while you wait for the fun to begin. But eventually, if I can't find it, you will tell me where to find the money."

He turned his attention to her small kitchen area. He opened the few pots and pans there. He overturned the boxes on the table, dumping the contents onto the floor. "All right, bitch. Enough game playing. It's time to get serious." He returned to the bed and climbed astride her again. "What's that? You're not sure how sharp my knife is? Let me show you." He pressed the tip of the knife to her abdomen and a small stream of blood started to ooze out. "See? Pretty sharp, huh? I don't think you want that knife slicing your neck now, do you? I'm going to remove that cloth in your mouth, and you will then tell me where to find your money. If you scream, I slice, and you die. Got that?"

She nodded.

With that, he pulled the cloth from her mouth.

She was unable to control herself. Her bloodcurdling scream pierced the silence, knowing that her life was about to end as the steel sliced open her neck. She did not even feel the slice. Instead, she opened her eyes, her heart pounding within her chest. Within seconds there was yelling outside her door. "Meranda, what's wrong? Are you all right?" It was the caretaker from downstairs. She grabbed a robe and went to the door.

"I'm sorry, Mr. Grinde," peeking her head through the door. "It was a horrible nightmare. I'm okay. I'm very sorry to have disturbed you."

"Okay, Meranda. Sorry about your bad dream. You really had me scared! Goodnight."

Meranda closed the door then slumped back against it. "Quel cauchemar!" she thought. After collecting herself a bit, she went to the kitchen in search of some whiskey to calm her nerves. The pounding in her heart continued relentlessly. She doubted that sleep would return tonight. How she wished that she could erase that St. Paul attacker from her memory. In her next visit to St. Paul she would have to get an update on his whereabouts. Hopefully, he had passed from this Earth to torment her no more.

Joy

Macie knocked on Meranda's door, but she was not there. Remembering that Meranda liked to sketch down by Commons beach, Macie decided to head there. As she approached the beach, a large dog ran up to her. Fortunately, it was apparently only seeking attention. Macie petted it before it was called away by a couple heading back from the beach. Sure enough. Meranda was seated on a bench down the beach a ways. As Macie walked up to her, she could see that Meranda had a sketchbook on her lap. She was sketching with a pencil.

"Hello, Meranda," Macie beamed as she sat down next to Meranda. "How are you this morning?"

"I'm fine now but I had a horrible sleep. I had the most awful nightmare. Remember that story I told all of you at the church tea?"

"Yes, of course."

"I dreamt that he was back and on the verge of killing me."

"I'm sorry to hear that. It'd be wonderful if you could forget about him. It'd be even better if he'd just go 'poof'!"

"Yes, but enough about me. You're certainly up and at 'em early!"

"I was too excited to sleep. I had to tell you about my adventure yesterday."

"Excellent! I'm all ears."

"Keith took me out yesterday in his canoe. Oh, Meranda, it was fun learning to paddle. We went all the way to Big Island! We tipped over just before landing at the island and Keith picked me up in his arms and carried me to shore. It was wonderful!" she exclaimed.

"I assume that you mean being carried in his arms?" asked her older friend.

"Yes. And he just grabbed me with a big kiss and told me he loved me. I did too," Macie exclaimed.

"Well, it sounds like you have found your man."

"It was such a wonderful day," Macie continued. "I just can't believe it. I took your advice and started my diary last night so that I don't forget the tiniest detail about that unbelievable experience."

"Great! You'll be really happy that you've done so."

"I can't really stay this morning. I've got a lot of work waiting for me at the hotel, but I couldn't wait to share this news with you."

"I'm honored. By the way, I'm heading back to St. Paul this morning for a few days to tend to a few things. Any chance you'd like to join me?"

"Oh, that'd be such fun, but I think we'll have to do that at another time. The approval of the park has launched a number of things in motion for Mr. Jerome and some of those things will involve me. I don't think I can go. Even though it's Sunday, I have to get a few things done at the hotel today."

"Well, I'm going to leave you with my address," writing on a little piece of paper, "just in case your schedule changes. You could come on over even for a day. I would love to show you around St. Paul."

"We'll see," Macie replied. "I hope you have a productive and enjoyable little trip. I'll really be looking forward to seeing you again when you get back."

Macie gave Meranda a hug, then headed for the hotel.

Observations

By the following morning, Macie had compiled even more paperwork related to hotel transactions with Vegas Thorpe, the Excelsior attorney. She now felt ready to take her observations to Mr. Jerome. She knew that he was at the hotel this morning.

"Good morning, Macie," he greeted her when she appeared at the door to his office. "Come on in," motioning to her to have a seat in the chair opposite his desk. "It looks like you've made good progress in getting that office under control."

"Yes, it's been challenging but I've just about got it licked. Mr. Adams has been very helpful in answering my questions."

"Good. What can I help you with this morning?"

"I've got some questions about the legal work being done by Vegas Thorpe."

"You've probably heard that Vegas came here as a member of my firm before he decided to set up his own practice in Excelsior. The hotel has become one of his major clients. What are you wondering about?"

"I'm curious about the large amount of money being spent by the hotel on his legal fees. Here are invoices from him. I've also created a separate list of payments to him," sliding documents across his desk towards him. "I found a number of inconsistencies, for example, instances where the hotel was billed for meetings which, according to Mr. Adams records, did not take place."

"Hmmm, that seems strange."

"There's more. It would appear that the hotel is being charged for continued work on property damage claims when the claims have already been settled."

"There must be some logical explanation. Why don't you let me take your records and ask Vegas about this? I'm heading over to Excelsior today so I should be able to meet with Vegas while I'm there."

"I'll finish putting together a little packet of materials for you for your meeting with Vegas. I'll be back in a few minutes."

After work the following day, Macie stopped by the Journal office to talk with Buzz on her way home. He was at his desk reviewing the latest edition of the paper.

"Hello, Macie. How's it going today?"

"Fine, thanks, but I've got some questions for you."

"Fire away."

"As you know, I've been going through a huge pile of paperwork out at the hotel. That paperwork raised some significant questions in my mind about Vegas Thorpe and the way he has been charging the hotel for his services."

"Tell me more."

"I shared my concerns with Mr. Jerome. He met with Vegas yesterday to raise some of the issues that I had flagged. After doing some checking of his records, Vegas agreed to issue a substantial credit to the hotel's account. I would say that Vegas is either dishonest or a bit careless in his billing practices."

"That's interesting, Macie. You're not the first to raise some questions about billing for his legal services. I've heard other businesspeople in town also raise some questions about him. But they hesitate to challenge him, given his status and the fact that he is so knowledgeable about the law."

"That makes me even more suspicious."

"I tell you what. Let's walk over to the bank and see if Bob Meier is still there. I know that he is one who has voiced some questions about Vegas' billing practices."

Together, they crossed Water Street after letting a wagon carrying a load of produce pass by in front of them. They entered the bank and spotted Bob Meier in his office at the back. They knocked at his door.

"Hello, folks. What can I do for you?" Meier inquired.

"Hello, Bob. I'm not sure if you have met my young friend here. This is Macie Stewart. She is doing some bookkeeping work for Mr. Jerome out at the St. Louis Hotel."

"It's nice to meet you, Miss Stewart. Please, have a seat."

"We're here because I remember a little conversation that we had a few weeks ago when you told me that the bank was starting to question legal fees being charged by Vegas Thorpe."

"Yes, I recall our conversation. And my feelings have not changed."

"Anyways, Macie shared similar observations on hotel billing with Mr. Jerome who took those concerns to Vegas. The end result is that the hotel is being issued a substantial credit for overcharges."

"All right, that does it. I thought that we were the only ones questioning his charges. Good for you, Miss Stewart, for bringing this to light. The bank has its own file of documentation in which we have summarized the discrepancies that we have noted. I also know that there are others in this town who have voiced similar concerns. It seems possible that Vegas may be 'cooking his books' a bit. I think we need to pay a visit to the sheriff."

The three of them headed for the sheriff's office.

When informed about the billing discrepancies and after briefly reviewing the bank's evidence shown to him, the sheriff shook his head. "I should be able to get a search warrant yet today. If I can, I'll pay a visit to Vegas first thing in the morning," the sheriff concluded. "Thanks for raising the issues with me." Everyone left the jail and headed for home as the workday was coming to a close.

It was time to try to put this traumatic day behind her. Upon entering the boarding house and seeing Mrs. O. and her warm, welcoming presence, Macie fell into her arms for a big hug. It had been an extraordinary day in Excelsior.

Floating

Sunshine flickered over the Commons beach as two good swimmers using strong crawl strokes suddenly stopped and stood up in chest-deep water.

Howard Jones exclaimed to his wife, "D'you see that?"

Smitty, now breathless, "Yes, I can't believe it! There's a body there just floating! We've gotta report this right away." They broke out of the water, running for the beach.

After hurriedly dressing, she shouted, "Let's go!"

They rushed to the sheriff's office, shouting, "Sheriff Herman, there's a body in the water! At Commons beach."

"Another drowning! There have been too many lately!" muttered the sheriff. "I'm on my way," he said, heading out the door with a stretcher.

The sheriff stopped by Buzz's office at the Journal to request assistance. The two of them, arriving soon at the beach, scanned the water and quickly spotted the body. The sheriff removed his boots then waded out to bring it back to shallow water and the two of them then lifted it onto the beach. This was the dead body of a woman, fully clothed. One look at her face, although distorted, and Buzz knew right away. It was Meranda, Macie's friend.

"Oh my gosh!" cried Buzz, "How can I tell Macie this awful news?"

The sheriff barely heard Buzz since his investigative mind had immediately kicked into gear. "Look there at her neck, Buzz. Those bluish, greenish marks are telling."

"What do you think, Sheriff?" Buzz replied, taking a closer look at the marks.

"I'd say she was strangled."

"That's awful!" Buzz replied, shaking his head.

"The neck bruises plus the fact that her body was still floating...she most likely didn't die from drowning. I'd say that she was killed then thrown into the water. And, as we saw, she was in the water facedown, not letting the air in her lungs to escape. Otherwise, her lungs would have taken on water, likely causing her to sink."

"Wow, Sheriff! You have learned a lot! What important observations!"

The sheriff paused, obviously still deep in thought. "I've seen several bodies retrieved from this lake. Some of those bodies had been in the lake a long time, others a very short time. I'd say that this one has not been in the water very long. Wrinkling of the skin in the hands has begun but it's not that significant yet. Adding all of this up, I would guess that her body has been in the lake less than one day. She was probably killed during the night and then thrown in the lake. Alright,

Buzz. Let's get her onto the stretcher and over to the undertaker. Then I'll get a telegraph message off to the county coroner."[19]

Bells

As Macie made her way down Water Street toward the docks to catch a boat to the hotel, a church bell a few blocks away began to ring. She found it odd that the ringing continued. After what seemed like several dozen rings, she noticed people stopping and huddling as if counting.

"Do you have any idea what all the ringing was about?" Macie asked two elderly women stopped along the street when the bell had suddenly quieted.

"In our town, when someone dies, the Covenant church bell is rung the number of times equal to their age. Apparently, someone about 50 years of age has just passed away" one of the women replied. They bowed their heads and the second woman added, "May heaven welcome the newly departed from our fair town. Amen."

As Macie resumed her walk, she noticed Buzz talking with two men half a block ahead of her.

"Buzz, a townsperson has just died?" As she approached him, his arms spread wide and he enveloped her in a hug. Macie started to tremble as his embrace without words signaled the devastating message about to be delivered.

"I'm very sorry, Macie, but Meranda is dead."

"No! NO!" Macie, aghast, cried out. "This can't be! How can you say this?" she said, bursting into tears, her body shaking all over.

"Unfortunately, it's true. I'll walk you over to join with Keith."

As Macie's sobs began to subside and her trembling eased, they walked in silence for a block or so. "What in the world happened to Meranda?" Macie asked, wiping the tears from her face.

"Her body was found just a short while ago by a young couple who'd been swimming off Commons beach. I hesitate to say more right now."

"Please tell me everything, Buzz. I need to know what happened."

"It would appear that she's been murdered."

"Murdered?! Who would possibly want to harm Meranda? This just seems impossible. I didn't even know that she had returned from St. Paul."

"The marks on her neck suggest she was strangled. She was then apparently thrown in the lake."

"How could anyone have been so devilish to murder her? No! This is too much! Please, God. Awaken me from this nightmare!"

As they rounded a corner, Keith appeared suddenly right in front of them.

"Macie, I'm so sorry!" Keith bleated, sweeping Macie into his arms.

"I'll take over from here, Buzz. Thank you very much. I'll walk Macie back to the boarding house."

"Let's walk to the church first, Keith," Macie blurted, barely getting the words out over the tears. "I need to have some time with God. How could He let this happen?"

Without saying more, they turned and began walking arm in arm toward the church.

Requiem

Macie dressed quickly in a black dress and headed for the boarding house door. She wanted to get to the church with plenty of time to spare.

"Just a second Dear," Mrs. O. called. She approached Macie, reaching out to hold her shoulders and give her a quick review. "You look very nice! I'm glad that dress fits you as well as it does."

"Thanks for letting me borrow it."

"My dear, Macie," Mrs. O. added, enveloping her in a warm hug. "I know this is a very painful loss for you. You run along now. I'll be there shortly myself."

The door to the church opened as Macie approached. It was Buzz who quickly gave Macie a hug. "Macie, Macie. I'm very sorry."

"Thank you, Buzz."

Mr. Jerome was standing just inside the door. He took Macie's arm and led her to a side room. "The pastor would like to meet briefly with key people. He will lead the group in a prayer before the start of the service. I'm sorry for your loss, Macie." Macie walked into the room and sat down next to Ella Severson to await the minister.

A few minutes later, the funeral service was underway. It was extremely hot and sticky at the Episcopal church as Macie listened to the minister. She watched beads of sweat drop from the nape of the parishioner in front of her.

"At this time, we call on Macie Stewart who would like to share some remembrances."

Macie walked up to the pulpit, depositing a book on the lectern.

"I come before you with mixed emotions this morning. I feel enormous grief over the loss of a woman who quickly became a dear friend. It's hard to believe that we knew each other for only a few weeks. Despite our age differences, we opened up to each other in ways that I have never done with anyone before. Meranda was a very wise woman with maternal instincts and a great companion whose presence inspired joy. I loved her dearly and I miss her."

Macie paused and began to shed tears as she struggled to find her next words. Keith walked up to the pulpit, put his arm around her, and encouraged her to take her time.

"I turned to Meranda for guidance in a variety of life's quandaries. A key piece of wisdom that I picked up from her related to the value of journaling. Meranda told me that she had been talking with herself via her diary for many years. She felt the process could be very helpful in gaining greater understanding about oneself. I'll share an entry from her diary in just a moment."

Macie took a deep breath then continued, "Meranda loved our community. While she came from St. Paul, she told me that she planned to settle in Excelsior permanently. She felt that this community could help her to make some progress in her personal life, to live a more righteous and respectful life. The women of this church led by Ella Severson reached out to Meranda, encouraging her to commit her life to Jesus. While Meranda resisted openly and vehemently at first, there were recently new signs of internal stirrings within her. I'd like to read to you the last entries from Meranda's diary, written just a few days before her death.

Friday, July 28

I attended another tea yesterday hosted by Ella Severson and some other church ladies. I feel a warmth within these women that is intriguing and very appealing. I really appreciate the kindly way they have reached out to me. I also appreciate their patience as I struggle with the message that they are sharing. They gave me two gifts during a tea today. They gave me a Bible that I have started to read for the first time. They also gave me a small pin in the shape of the cross with my initials engraved on it. I have added the pin to my favorite scarf. These kind women have encouraged me to ask the Lord to help me to come to know Him –

something that I have never considered – until now.

Dear God —
This is perhaps the start of a new chapter in my life. It is the first time that I am trying to pray. Please, God, help me to come to know you. You are central in the lives of many new friends who I respect. If you are real, I would like to weave you into my life. Thank you for listening to me. Amen

Macie paused and gathered her composure. "May you rest in peace, my dear friend. I pray God has welcomed you into His heavenly kingdom."

The organist responded with a beautiful prelude. The congregation then joined in and a stirring rendition of the hymn "Abide With Me" filled the church and spilled out the open windows into the surrounding neighborhood. Tears flowed freely in Excelsior.

After a brief homily and a couple more hymns, the ceremony ended. Mr. Jerome approached Macie afterwards. "I'm so sorry, Macie. This has been so stressful for you. With all the fabulous work that you have done for us, you clearly deserve some time off. Please feel free to take whatever time you need."

"Thank you very much, Mr. Jerome."

Adventure

Grieving after the terrible loss of Meranda, Macie sat on her bed resolved to find new friends and outdoor activity that would help her to heal. One venture that Keith had mentioned stuck in her mind. Sailing! Oh, joy! Occasionally she had seen sailboats gracefully gliding their way out on the big lake.

How could she take part? She knew that Buzz and his pals had been talking about racing. She jumped up and rushed for the dock. Buzz was there busily photographing a big ferry boat just entering the harbor.

"Buzz," she cried. "I want to go sailing. Any possibility that I can get involved?" she pleaded.

"Maybe, but you know it's mostly men who are sailing."

Still, Macie felt persistent today and went to find Keith who was probably also down at another marina. She soon found him. "Are you going to be racing today, Keith?"

"Yes, I am." Keith had recently become a member of the Minnetonka yacht club.

"Do you think there is any chance you might need another crew member – meaning me?"

"I don't know, Macie. I have my crew pretty much set. And I don't think women usually sail but stick around and we'll see."

Keith was the skipper of a small racing catboat loaded with sandbags for ballast, a boat often called simply a sandbagger.

As the day was already very windy and was becoming even windier, Keith had notified his crew of four men, all different weights, warning them to be prepared for big winds.

As they were entering the final stages of their race preparations, Keith announced: "I think we need even more weight today, guys. So, Macie is here and wants to go and we need her."

Keith explained directions to her first. "The crew's job is to balance the boat and when our big wooden boom with its huge sail moves suddenly from one side to the other, all crew members must duck their heads and move to the other side -- fast! Got that, Macie?"

She nodded and stepped gingerly into the boat sitting exactly where he told her. Wearing a lengthy coatdress, she felt a little impeded but was determined to follow the skipper's directions. Next, they headed for the course where Keith joined the other catboats lining up for the race.

Soon, she heard a gun go off, startling her already shaky nerves. No one had mentioned that at all. Seeing Macie startle, Keith yelled out: "Macie, once the judge shoots that gun into the air, that means it's time for their fleet to cross the starting line and head for the first mark." As the boat swung into position, the crew ducked and moved to the opposite side.

"Whew!" thought Macie. "I'm actually racing now."

About twenty minutes later, they were sailing past the Pillsbury Estate. Macie couldn't help peeking to see whether Mrs. Pillsbury[20] was watching. Just at that moment, Keith jibed the sailboat and, as the boat turned, a blast of wind hit launching Macie and two other crew members overboard. Keith immediately turned the boat directly into the wind and held it there to stop it to the best of his ability. The three crew members started to swim towards the boat. Despite her heavy clothing, Macie got back to the boat first. Quickly she was grabbed and lifted, dress and all, back up into the boat. The other two crew members then reached the boat and managed to crawl back aboard. With the soggy clothes under an overcast sky, Macie began shivering. She assumed they would head back home because of her but the race had not yet ended. To her dismay, she learned there was no such thing as quitting in a sailing race unless there was some grave danger. Keith quickly ordered everyone into their positions and headed for the final mark. A short time later, the race ended. Not surprisingly, they came in last.

"Oh Keith," cried Macie. "I'm so sorry I ruined the race for you."

Keith, huddling with her in his dry jacket, tried to comfort her, "Macie, sweetie. You didn't ruin the race for us. You weren't alone in falling out of the boat. The other two who also went overboard are both very experienced sailors. It happens! Furthermore, you got back to the boat faster than they did. You did well today. And now that you've got experience, I'm confident you'll be invited to crew again."

As they slowly cruised toward shore, Keith decided to anchor alongside the new Minnetonka Yacht Club clubhouse, designed by popular architect, Harry Wild Jones. He wanted to show it off to Macie as an expression of the latest and best in architecture. And no wonder! The wood frame structure soared into the sky with a fantastic roof of several gabled peaks that billowed out like actual sails over the base. "No wonder you're so proud of this club," gasped Macie.

That evening, lying in bed back at the boarding house, Macie was reflective. What a day! She had learned something new and different, a sport that engages your mind as well as your physical skills.

Also, Macie now realized that this mighty lake, Lake Minnetonka, could be not only serene and beautiful, but at times wild and powerful.

As she thought further about the eventful day, she suddenly felt a twinge of guilt at having had such a good time the day after Meranda's funeral. However, she knew in her heart that Meranda would have wanted her to go on living her life to the fullest. "Thank you, Meranda, for the important life lessons you shared with me." And with that thought, she rolled over and drifted off to sleep.

Discussion

Mrs. O. hustled to the door and was surprised to see Sheriff Herman on the doorstep.

"Hello, Elizabeth. Is Macie here?"

"Why yes, I believe she is. Just a second, please."

Mrs. O. headed upstairs and returned shortly with Macie.

"Hello, Sheriff. What can I do for you?" Macie asked.

"Why don't we step out on the porch for a few minutes so we can talk privately."

"Sure, Sheriff."

After the two of them had sat down, the sheriff continued: "I'm sorry about the loss of your friend, Meranda. I believe you were her best friend in town. I need to ask you a few questions."

"Okay, Sheriff."

"Where were you on the night of the murder. Sorry, but I need to be complete in my investigation."

"I understand, Sheriff. I was with Keith. We had dinner at his apartment then we did a moonlight canoe ride along the shore to the west."

"Okay. Keep going, Macie. Tell me more. When were you out on the lake?"

"We probably headed out onto the lake about 9 o'clock. We parked for a while on a little beach we found and then paddled back late. I would guess we came back around midnight. Then Keith walked me home to the boarding house."

"Hmmm. That would mean that you canoed past Commons beach, right?"

"Yes, we did."

"Tell me more. Where did you canoe with respect to the shore?"

"On the way there, we were fairly far out in the lake to get a good view of the moon as it was rising. On our way back, we hugged the shoreline."

"Do you remember seeing anyone or any activity as you passed Commons beach?"

"Actually, now that I think about it, we did hear some splashing on our way there. We looked over and saw someone in the water. We couldn't see very well given how dark it was, but we assumed that it was someone out for a late-night swim. Ooohhh, I should've thought of that. It could have been the murderer!"

"Yes, that's true. I will have to talk with Keith to corroborate your account of the evening. Do you know of other people in town who Meranda had been associating with of late?"

"As far as I know, she really didn't socialize much yet in town. She had met with some of the church ladies. As you recall, she was introduced to several locals at the recent dinner here at the boarding house. And come to think of it, she had some fun dancing with Vegas Thorpe at the St. Louis Hotel ball recently. That's all I can think of now."

"Yeah, I've questioned Vegas from his jail cell. Yes, he's been arrested. He claims that he was at home by himself that evening. Given that he was almost always at home alone in the evening, it would be hard to prove otherwise. Can you think of anyone else that I could question?"

"Meranda told a little story to some of the church ladies recently about an assault that she experienced sometime in the past over in St. Paul. That guy might be harboring a grudge."

"That sounds plausible. He'd be a potential suspect. Anyone else?"

"Sorry, Meranda never really mentioned anyone else. But here's an idea for you, Sheriff. Meranda kept a diary. If she was seeing other people, her diary might mention them."

"Good idea, Macie. Let's you and I go over to her apartment and look at her diary."

"All right, Sheriff. I'm happy to assist."

They walked to Meranda's apartment and Macie quickly located the diary. Macie turned to the end of the book. Together she and the sheriff worked backward, quickly reviewing the entries, of which there were very few that had been written during her recent weeks in Excelsior. None of the entries dealt with Excelsior residents. No entries had been made since Meranda left town days earlier for St. Paul.

"I'm sorry, Sheriff. The diary is not going to be helpful to you in your investigation."

"It was a good thought, Macie. I'm going to go talk with Keith now."

Wayzata

"I still can't believe that she's gone," Macie lamented. She pulled her coat closer to her as a gust of wind sailed thru the cabin of the ferry as they cruised north toward Wayzata.

"The sheriff is so dang busy we'll see if we can't figure out what happened to her. It didn't take me too long to identify our first suspect," Buzz noted. "I asked a few people around town if they had noticed anything or anyone unusual around the day of her death."

"What did you find out?"

"Several of them, including Mr. Jimmy[21], mentioned an unidentified stranger who was seen in town late in the afternoon the day before her body was found. The guy was just hanging around and didn't seem to have anything to do. He was pretty noticeable as he was well over six feet tall with a heavy black beard. He seemed to have disappeared by the morning of the discovery of her body."

"Okay, so what leads us to Wayzata?"

"I checked with a few hotels in town, and Charlie Holmdale at the White House Hotel[22] said this sounds like a fellow who had spent the night at their hotel. Apparently, the guy checked in late in the afternoon, left the hotel for an hour or so in the evening, then returned for the night. Gary Anderson is the guy's name. Charlie said that Anderson mentioned that he and his wife had had a big argument and he needed some time and space for her to cool off. The guy cited a Wayzata address upon checking in. Charlie also found out that he is employed by Moore Boatworks. It shouldn't be too hard to check out his story."

A half hour later, Buzz and Macie debarked on the other side of the lake in Wayzata, a picturesque town that was thriving in part due to James J. Hill's railroad and the booming boat building business. A quick inquiry with the dock attendant pointed them in the direction of the home at 63 Lake Street. "Let's just walk through his neighborhood," Buzz suggested. "The ideal would be to find a neighbor outside we could talk with."

Crossing the railroad tracks that ran along the waterfront reminded Buzz about a story that Macie had probably not heard.

"Have you heard about James J. Hill and his railroad, Macie?"

"Yes, a bit. Why?"

"These are the tracks. There has been some long-standing friction between Hill and Wayzata."

"What's the problem?" Macie inquired.

"Sometime in the 80's, the town wanted Hill to move his railroad tracks back 300 feet from the lake.

Hill was furious that a little town would challenge his mighty railroad. So, he punished the town by moving the depot about a mile to the east. People here have quite a hike to do to catch a train."

"Wow!"

"Apparently, the relationship has improved. I've heard that Hill is going to build a new depot back in town. They also say that it may be the nicest depot anywhere within his system."

Macie and Buzz continued walking. They found the house a few blocks from the docks. They were in luck. A neighbor two doors down was beating rugs on her clothesline.

"Hello, Ma'am," Buzz shouted. "Would you mind a couple of questions about your neighborhood?"

"Okay," the woman shouted back. "What would you like to know?"

Buzz and Macie approached the house a bit but continued to shout. "A family friend from Wisconsin is interested in moving to Wayzata and we are checking out neighborhoods that might be of interest."

The woman quit working on her rugs and started toward Buzz and Macie.

"Our friend is an author who would work out of his house. Peace and quiet are of utmost importance. How would you rate this neighborhood on that?"

"In general, Wayzata is a very peaceful town," the woman replied without hesitation. She looked down the street in both directions then lowered her voice, as if to continue with more confidence. "Yes, while Wayzata is peaceful, I can't say that our neighbors two doors down are great on that count. Those two have some doozies of arguments. Some of those arguments are very loud and easily overheard with the windows open. There was a classic example a couple days ago. Oh, I don't know. Maybe I should not say more."

"If you wouldn't mind, please continue," Buzz requested. "We really appreciate your insights and we won't share anything you say with others."

"Okay," the woman shrugged. "I think it was Tuesday afternoon. Those two were yelling back and forth until the husband slammed the front door in a huff and took off, yelling that he was going to spend the night somewhere else while his wife cooled down. I'm confident that everyone on the block heard that argument."

"Wow!" Buzz noted.

"So, if peacefulness of the neighborhood is top priority, as long as those two are here or until they change their ways, your friend might be advised to seek a different neighborhood."

"I see," Buzz replied. "Thank you very much, Ma'am. We appreciate your honest guidance."

"That was too easy. Anderson's story checks out perfectly so far," Macie noted as they walked away.

"Let's go to Moore Boatworks[23] to see if we can spot Anderson. Perhaps we could chat with him."

Moore Boatworks was located on the lake just a short distance away. There were a variety of boats in various stages of completion around the grounds. Several employees could be seen putting finishing touches on boats apparently about ready for delivery. At the far end of the grounds, one such employee fit the description of Mr. Anderson. Macie and Buzz headed in his direction.

"Good afternoon," Buzz said.

Anderson looked up from the finishing work that he was doing. "Hello," Anderson replied.

"These are sure beautiful boats!" Macie noted.

"Yup. Our boats rank amongst the best in the entire country," Anderson said, smiling proudly. "You can find our boats on just about every major body of water across America," Anderson continued.

"We would like to ask you a couple of questions, if you don't mind," Buzz continued.

"Well, I'll decide if I feel like answering depending on what you ask. What's up?" Anderson replied.

"We're not police. I'm a reporter for the *Excelsior Journal* and Macie, here, works at the St. Louis Hotel. But we're investigating what appears to have been a murder in Excelsior. She was a friend of ours," Buzz explained. "Have you heard about that?"

"Yes, I did. People in town have been talking about it. Are you telling me that I'm a suspect?"

"You were in town last Tuesday, right?" queried Macie. "That was the night of the murder."

"That's the night I was there all right but I ain't no murderer!" Anderson was glaring and turning red in the face.

"Would you mind telling us why you were in town?" Macie asked.

"Well, if you gotta know. Yeah. Me and my wife had a big fight. I needed to get away from her for a while. So, I came down here, got one of our boats, and cruised over to Excelsior for the night."

"And what did you do in Excelsior?" Macie continued.

"I just killed some time traipsing around town for a while. I stayed at the White House. Went out for a bite to eat at Hardy's. Hit the sack early 'cause I had to be back at work early the next morning."

"Your story checks out perfectly, Mr. Anderson. We're sorry for having to put you on the spot but we appreciate your willingness to help us in our investigation," Buzz replied, offering his hand to shake Anderson's.

Anderson reciprocated but added, "Geez, folks, you sure had me riled there for a second. Thank God you believe me! I ain't perfect but I certainly ain't a murderer."

"We'll tell the Excelsior sheriff that your story checks out. We won't interrupt you any further from your work. And we'll keep our eyes peeled around the lake for your company's boats."

"You won't have to look very hard. They're everywhere!" Anderson said and returned his attention to the lacquer he was applying.

Macie and Buzz started to walk away.

"Well, it seems highly unlikely that he had anything to do with Meranda's death. He seems like a decent fellow who has no problem telling about his recent stay in

Excelsior. Everything about his story is consistent," Macie muttered to Buzz as they headed for the docks to catch the next steamer back to Excelsior.

Together, they decided that, given Meranda's recent stay in St. Paul, perhaps a trip there would be appropriate to continue their investigation.

While riding across the lake back to Excelsior, Macie turned to Buzz. "You seem tense about something. I sense that something's bothering you."

"I'm steamed up."

"About what?"

"My wife said that she wants a part-time job."

"Doing what?"

"Assisting Doc Phillips, the veterinarian."

"Hmmm…what leads her to think about doing that?"

"I really don't want to talk about it today. I just told her 'Absolutely not! My wife is not going to work outside our home. Period!'"

Macie silently scanned the lake.

"Can't you see that this would be impossible?" Buzz asked.

"Hmmm...I'm not sure that I can just agree with that without hearing more of the details."

"Really! Society clearly rules that the husband's the family head. The Bible says something along the same line. And almost all wives that I know stay home to run the household and care for the children. Bottom line: this should be my decision!"

"Sorry, Buzz. I'd be happy to talk about your dilemma if and when you are more open to talking about it and a bit more flexible in your thinking."

"You've really surprised me, Macie. I can't handle more on this topic today," turning his attention to a distant view across the lake.

St. Paul

Macie and Buzz climbed aboard the trolley car, deposited ten cents each in the box and took their seats for the ride to St. Paul. With a clang of the bell, the trolley car started off on its journey, an occasional spark from the electric line overhead reminding all aboard of the newfangled power source for the car.[24]

"This is exciting!" exclaimed Macie as the trolley car accelerated quickly and soon left the town behind.

"It certainly is! What a boon to Excelsior this new system is going to be for the town and the new park!" Buzz added. They sat silently for a while, marveling as the car zipped along through the forest surrounding the lake then through the surrounding countryside.

Buzz excused himself and stepped out on the platform for a smoke.

Macie sat alone and enjoyed watching the constantly changing scenery as forests and ponds and the occasional farm streamed by. Her thoughts then turned to the wide differences in the nature of her mission, seeking information about the murder of her dear friend, and the mundane activities of the people she saw from the window: a man driving a wagon, a small cloud of dust trailing behind; children playing behind a farm house, freezing in place momentarily to wave at the trolley as it rattled by; a buggy coming down another road, a basket of melons visible between the couple. Thinking again about her fact-finding mission, she prayed: "The Lord bless us and keep us on our way and bring us safely through!"

Buzz rejoined her as the trolley slowed to a stop in the town of Hopkins to take on more passengers. Once streaming along again, the two sat largely in silence, enjoying the views as the car gradually approached Minneapolis. After passing Lake Harriet on the right and Lake Calhoun on the left, the two descended on Lake Street in order to transfer to the line running straight east to St. Paul.

Twenty minutes later they were entering downtown St. Paul.

"Hey, Macie. Look up there," Buzz noted, pointing to the up the hill to the north. "Isn't it majestic?"

"Beautiful!"

"That's our new state capitol building."[25] The new building, designed by St. Paul architect Cass Gilbert, loomed over the capitol hill with a glorious marble façade topped by golden horses in formation.

The trolley soon came to a stop and they exited.

Macie pulled out a small piece of paper. "Meranda's house is at 18 West 8th Street." She asked a man passing by if he could point them in that direction. "Sure, it's just a few blocks up that way," as he gestured to the right.

A few minutes later, Macie and Buzz stood before the handsome stone house. "This looks to be the place," Macie noted. They approached and knocked on the door. No one answered. They returned to the street and looked around. They could see the spires of a large church about a block to the north. They decided to go there to inquire further.

Macie and Buzz entered the Church of the Assumption and looked around, eventually finding the office where an elderly woman was dealing with some paperwork.

"Excuse us, Ma'am. Do you know the neighborhood?" Buzz inquired.

"To some degree, yes," the woman replied. "I've lived near here for the past ten years."

"We're looking for the residence of Meranda Delaquila. We were told that she lives at 18 West 8th Street just a block to the south," Buzz continued.

"I don't recognize that name," the woman replied. "But that is an address that many St. Paul residents know because its owner is frequently mentioned in the newspapers. But there must be some mistake in your information as that residence does not belong to a Meranda."

"That's very curious," Buzz continued. "Who does own that house?"

"It's owned by Louise Robinson, simply known as 'Mrs. Robinson' to most in our town," the woman replied. "I've never heard of a woman by the name you cited. Perhaps you were given inaccurate information."

"No, my friend Macie here was given that information by Meranda herself. Could you by chance describe Louise Robinson's appearance?"

"Yes, she is rather tall and about 45 - 50 years old. She has a trace of a French accent. She usually wears a very distinctive artistic comb holding the back of her hair."

Macie and Buzz looked at each other in astonishment as the description fit perfectly with Meranda.

"I believe that Mrs. Robinson is vacationing somewhere for the summer which would explain why no one answered the door at her home. However, I'm not comfortable in saying anything more about her. If you want to learn more, I would encourage you to visit one of the newspapers, either the *Pioneer Press* or the *Dispatch*. You can learn a lot about her in either of those papers.

The office of the *Pioneer Press* is just up the street a couple of blocks."

"Thank you very much, Ma'am. You have been very helpful," Macie noted as she and Buzz headed for the exit.

"That was very strange. Do you think that Meranda isn't her real name? If so, why would she hide her identity from us? And why would this Louise Robinson or Meranda or whatever her name is be frequently mentioned in the local newspapers?" Macie queried.

"Let's go find out," Buzz responded. "Let's visit the *Pioneer Press* office next," said Buzz. "Whoever we talk to there will undoubtedly want to know why we're inquiring about this Louise Robinson. I think it might make sense for us to say that she has disappeared for a few days. Telling them the full truth will create a big news event that may make it harder for us to get more insights."

Macie and Buzz soon spotted the *Pioneer Press* office and walked in. They were greeted by a young man seated at a desk in the front of the office. There were two other men at work in the office and printing machinery could be seen through a door at the back of the office.

"Can I help you?" the young man inquired.

"Yes, we're seeking information about a resident who lives just a couple of blocks from here, Louise Robinson. A woman at the Church of the Assumption told us that Louise Robinson is well known in St. Paul and that she is frequently mentioned in newspaper articles," Buzz replied.

"Sure, I can help you with that. But I'm curious as to why you're seeking information about her."

Buzz continued: "Louise Robinson has been vacationing in our town, Excelsior, out on Lake Minnetonka. She's been there for most of the summer. She disappeared recently and we're concerned about her. She told us that she hails from St. Paul so we thought that we might learn things here that could help us to locate her."

"Okay. Why don't you have a seat," the man continued, motioning to the two chairs by his desk. "By the way, I'm Tim Foley," extending his hand.

"I'm Buzz Greenfield and this is my friend, Macie Stewart. We're pleased to make your acquaintance." They shook hands with Foley then sat down.

Foley continued: "I'm a bit uncomfortable in telling you about Mrs. Robinson in the presence of a lady. So, if Miss Stewart would like to go for a stroll, that might be preferable."

Macie, smiling, replied: "I appreciate your gesture, Mr. Foley, but I would prefer to hear whatever it is that you have to say. All that matters to me is that we learn whatever we can that will help us to find our friend."

"Understood. As you wish," Foley replied. "Mrs. Robinson was St. Paul's most successful madam[26] in running a house of ill fame."

"A house of ill fame?" Macie inquired.

"That is the most common expression used in St. Paul. A brothel. A house of prostitution."

"Oh my!" Macie sighed.

"Sorry. I'm not sure how much you want to know about Mrs. Robinson's past," Foley added and paused.

"No, please go on, Mr. Foley," Macie replied. "While it may be somewhat painful to hear, we want to learn everything we can about the background of our friend. She has always been somewhat vague about her life in St. Paul. I think we now understand why. But something within this information just might help us to locate her."

"All right. Well that industry is alive and well in St. Paul," Foley continued. "There are over a half dozen brothels in operation at the present time and many smaller operations. Louise Robinson ran the largest brothel here for years, generally employing six to eight inmates, the term often used for the prostitutes."

Macie gulped at hearing this new and disturbing information presented so matter-of-factly.

"There were reasons for which her brothel was the largest. Louise had a reputation as an excellent employer. Her inmates were highly compensated and treated very well. There was very little turnover in her operation."

"Well, at least that's good to know," Macie replied.

"While there are St. Paulites, particularly within the religious community, who believe that prostitution should be stamped out, the city has adopted policies that seem to work well. The city seeks to regulate the industry. Technically, the madams are violating the laws so, as lawbreakers, they're arrested each month. They make an appearance in court as a group, they're fined, then they're released to return to their establishments. We typically cover those court proceedings in our paper."

"It's hard to imagine our friend involved in prostitution," Buzz noted.

"You'll notice that I said that Mrs. Robinson 'ran' a house of ill fame," Foley continued. "The city changed its policies for a time a few years ago in an attempt at prohibition. Mrs. Robinson responded by closing her brothel and auctioning off her brothel's furnishings. The city's attempt at prohibition lasted only about three months before it was judged to be a failure. The city quickly resumed its old methods for merely regulating the industry. But Louise Robinson didn't reopen her establishment. Instead she began investing in real estate."

"Good for Meranda," muttered Macie.

"Is there anything else that you feel we should know about Louise Robinson?" Buzz asked.

"Yes, there was a series of events that riveted our city over the course of a year, a few years back."

"Please go on, Mr. Foley. You're being extremely helpful," Macie noted.

"A few years ago, while Mrs. Robinson was still running her brothel, the owner of St. Paul's largest gambling hall, George Crummey, showed up very late one night at the brothel and demanded wine, which Mrs. Robinson refused him. They started to argue, and the confrontation soon turned physical as Crummey started to assault her. Mrs. Robinson hit him with a rolling pin then quickly escaped to her residence next door. But within a few minutes, her brothel was on fire. That fire spread quickly and soon spread to her residence as well. Despite the efforts of the fire department who were on the scene quickly, both wooden buildings burned to the ground."

Macie thought to herself that the story was clearly the long version of the one that Meranda had related to the church ladies.

"Was anyone killed or injured in the fire?" Buzz asked.

"No, but since Mrs. Robinson's buildings were nice and were elegantly furnished, her material losses were pretty significant. She sued Crummey in civil court for damages, for about $30,000 if I recall correctly. The trial went on for about four days and we reported on the proceedings each day in our paper. The trial ended in a hung jury."

"From what you have told us, it sounds like the fire did not end Mrs. Robinson's tenure as a madam," Buzz noted.

"Correct. She rebuilt her buildings, this time in stone, and resumed her business for a few more years until her retirement that I have already mentioned."

"Mrs. Robinson was back in town recently. Any chance that you know what she was doing during her brief stay here?" Macie asked.

"Sorry, I have no idea. I had heard that she was vacationing somewhere for the summer. That's the last I heard about her," Foley responded.

"So, it's been a few years since Mrs. Robinson closed her brothel. How is her relationship now with the rest of the community?" Buzz asked.

"I would say that, while everyone knows of her past, the community has been very accepting of her. She keeps a low profile and seems to be doing well with her real estate investments. In my opinion, she is a respected member of our community," Foley added.

"Do you know if she has any immediate family?" Buzz asked.

"I don't know anything about her family," Foley replied.

"Do you happen to know if she has any close friends in town?" Buzz continued.

"Yes, she has a good friend who is also a former madam, Lois Fredericks. I believe that she rents a room from the owner of the Hill Town Cafe over on Market Street," Foley added.

"Is there anything else that you feel we should know?" Macie asked.

"No, I can't think of anything else. Also, I should probably get back to work," Foley noted as he rose to shake hands. "But, if I can be of any further assistance, please don't hesitate to come back. Furthermore, I'd be interested in hearing the end results of your search, in case there's a story there that we would want to publish. Good luck to you in finding your friend."

"Thanks a lot, Mr. Foley," Buzz replied. "You've been very helpful."

While Macie and Buzz were gone, Keith missed his sweetheart so much, he had a hard time carrying out his work on the Big Island park. The contractor and crew had cleared a large section of land for the picnic grounds and, using wood from the felled trees, built a good-sized pavilion for picnickers. Meanwhile, Keith had worked out his design plan with the lighting expert who would soon craft the lighting tower, slated to be one of the chief attractions of the new park.

Going back and forth on a ferry boat taking him regularly to the island, Keith had grown to know the captain. His name was Jerry, an attractive middle-aged bachelor, known for chasing local women. Together, they laughed at Jerry's adventures until one day, he happened to mention the newest "glamour girl" in town, Meranda.

Keith perked up asking, "Oh, yes, she's quite the talk of the town. Have you dated her?"

"I first met her when she came on my moonlight cruise. Then as we got better acquainted, I saw her several times. She really knew her way around. She had some big city airs 'cuz she came here from St. Paul. So, we drank a little bit together and talked a lot. She has a nice small apartment with a cozy bedroom," grinned Jerry.

"Did you happen to see her the other night?" asked Keith, clearly referring to the night of the murder that, by now, was known to all.

"Well I don't keep track like that. Things just sort of happen when you fall for a woman," seeming to indicate he didn't want to talk about it further.

Keith dropped his line of questioning and thought that maybe Macie and Buzz should talk to Jerry too. He might well be considered a suspect, considering that he was so vague about the night of Meranda's death and that he admitted having spent time socializing and drinking with her.

As they left the *Pioneer Press* office, Buzz pointed to a bench across the street. "Let's sit down over there and talk through what we have learned."

"Good idea."

"I'm stunned!" Macie began. "While it would have been nice to learn that Meranda had been in some other line of work, I'm not surprised that she was very successful."

"Agreed," Buzz replied. "You know, come to think of it, there was a potential suspect revealed just now by Foley: that Crummey, the guy who burned down Mrs. Robinson's buildings. He probably had a good-sized chip on his shoulder over being sued and taken to court."

"You're right!" Macie replied. "We should've asked more about him. Let's see if Foley knows where we could find him today."

They quickly walked back across the street and entered the office.

"You're back already!" Foley retorted, smiling from his desk.

"One more quick question for you, please," Macie replied. "Do you happen to know where we could find this Mr. Crummey?"

"I can understand how you might want to talk with him. Unfortunately, he moved away about a year ago. Business at his gambling hall had been steadily declining, probably in part due to the negative press from the trial. He closed his business and left. I think he went to Duluth but I'm not sure about that."

"Thank you again, Mr. Foley." Buzz replied.

"You're very welcome. Good luck in your search for your friend," Foley noted, as he returned his focus to a document on his desk.

Outside the *Pioneer Press* office, "Let's see if we can find that Lois Fredericks," Buzz noted. "I think we passed Market Street over that way," he said, pointing left.

Within minutes, they had found the cafe.

"Excuse me, Ma'am," Macie asked the woman at the counter. "Do you know where we can find Lois Fredericks?"

"You're in luck. That's her over there at the end of the counter. Hey, Lois," she shouted. "You've got visitors."

Macie and Buzz approached the slightly stout middle-aged woman, who greeted them with a welcoming smile.

"Have a seat folks," she said gesturing to two open seats at the counter next to her. "What can I do for you?"

"We're friends of Louise Robinson who has been visiting our town of Excelsior this summer. She has disappeared recently, so we' re concerned about her. We need information that might help us find her. According to the reporter at the *Pioneer Press*, you're a friend of Louise's, is that right?"

"Yes, that's correct. I consider her my best friend. She was just back in town a few days ago. We had dinner together and had a good chance to catch up on things. I don't suppose that you're Macie," she inquired, looking at Macie.

"Yes, I'm Macie," she replied.

"Louise told me a bit about you and your new friendship. She's really enjoyed getting to know you."

Holding back a tear, Macie replied: "I feel the same about her. That's why we want to try to figure out where she might be. Did she mention anything unusual to you? Was there anything bothering her? Do you happen to know why she returned to St. Paul for those days?"

"She told me that she had some business to tend to with the bank regarding her real estate holdings. She also just wanted to check on her house. But she seemed to be very much her normal pleasant self. If she had been under stress for any reason, I'm sure she would have told me about it. Sorry that I can't be of more help to you. I'd be happy to send you a telegram if she shows up here in the next few days."

"That would be most helpful," Buzz replied. "You could send it to me, Buzz Greenfield. I work for the newspaper in town. The telegraph operator there knows where to find me."

"Well, I hope that Louise shows up soon," Mrs. Fredericks continued. "You've gotten me concerned."

"We'll do our best to find her," Macie replied. "Thank you very much for your insights."

Macie and Buzz rose and headed for the door. Once outside, Buzz reflected: "Well, I'm thinking that we've perhaps reached our conclusion here in St. Paul. We can't completely rule out Crummey as a suspect, but it sounds like he has moved pretty far away. And I'm not sensing anyone else from St. Paul as our suspect – at least so far."

"Agreed," Macie replied. "We've learned a lot about Meranda or Louise, but she seems to have been on good terms with just about everyone over here. Let's check on the next streetcar back home."

They were soon aboard a streetcar headed west.

After watching the sights for a while as they rode along, Buzz broke the silence. "Macie, I've been doing some more thinking about my wife working outside our home."

"Okay. I'm still curious as to what it is that leads your wife to think about assisting a veterinarian."

"She has always had an affinity with animals. It started when she was about 8 years old. One lamb in a set of twins on their farm was abandoned by its mother. Her dad turned the lamb's care over to Sarah."

"And how did it go?"

"My wife loved it. The lamb bonded with her as if she was its mother. The lamb did very well! You'll have to ask my wife sometime about her 'Molly the Lamb' story. She loves to tell it."

"I will ask her."

"That was just the first of many experiences on their farm where my wife's involvement with their animals had positive impact on their health. My wife loved helping her Dad with the animals – all of them."

"If I'm not mistaken, I believe that veterinarians assist mainly with horses, right?"

"That's true. Farmers tend to take care of the other animals themselves."

"Did your wife get any experience with tending to horses on their farm?"

"Yes, she did – a lot of it. From an early age, she was tasked with taking their horses to Babb's Iger for shoeing. He kind of took her under his wing and taught her a lot about the shoeing process."

"She sounds pretty qualified to me."

"Babbs also provides other horse care services and he allowed Sarah to watch it all. Anyways, she said that she really misses those experiences with animals. She would like to weave more of them into her life."

"There's nothing better than going to work in a field that one is passionate about."

"I suppose that's true. But she's busy enough taking care of our home."

"Your kids are pretty independent, right?"

"Yes, they're teenagers now. But, if my wife is at work, who is going to cook our meals? Who is going to iron my shirts?"

"Buzz, do you really think that men are incapable of learning to do some simple cooking?"

"I suppose not. But, that's women's work."

"Says who?"

"Everybody knows that."

"I think it would be better if both spouses share household chores. I'm confident that you would not need to starve to death during the occasional times that your wife is working."

"Hmmm."

"Is ironing too difficult for you? Ironing is not much fun or very rewarding. Why should the burden fall only on women?"

"All right, I get your point. But this feels like an assault on my manhood. It's the man's role to be the breadwinner in the family."

"You would still be a breadwinner. And wouldn't some additional income be of value to your family?"

"That's very true. We're forever just scraping by. All right, all right. I'll give this whole topic more thought. Macie, you're really a stitch, y'know?"

Macie smiled.

Collaboration

Early the next morning, Keith called on Macie at the boarding house. "Macie, my love, "said Keith with a welcoming hug. "Tell me what you learned in St. Paul about our friend."

"Oh, Keith, Meranda is not her real name! Her real name is Louise Robinson. And she used to be a Madam!"

"Oh, wow! Really?"

"I didn't even know what that meant but now I do. Imagine, that city has a whole neighborhood of these brothels -- and Meranda operated one," gushed Macie, trying hard to swallow. Keith realized that his dear young friend had no idea of prostitution and how widespread it is.

"Well now you know, Dear. On the other hand, remember Meranda told you she was planning to change her life and that's probably why she came to Excelsior."

"Yes, that's exactly what she told me," replied Macie, "and I still loved her."

"Of course, you did," Keith reassured her. "Did you find evidence of a suspect in her murder over in St. Paul?"

"Only one – at least so far. The guy who assaulted her years ago might still be considered a suspect although he has moved to Duluth. We met with several people who convinced us that Louise Robinson, who will forever be 'Meranda' to us, was now a respected member of the community without any apparent enemies."

"Would you like to hear what I know of a possible suspect here?" He then described the ferry boat driver as a good-looking womanizer who drove Meranda around on these moonlight cruises. "He probably got drunk one night while trying to romance her, grew angry and when she didn't respond, he strangled her and threw her overboard," figured Keith.

"Was it the same night that she was murdered?" asked Macie.

"I think so. Should we go to the sheriff with this story?" Keith suggested.

"Yes, I'll get Buzz and we'll all go," Macie sighed.

Dutifully, they headed off to find Buzz and see the sheriff.

"Sheriff, knowing that you're so busy with problems here in town like that knifing and the school burning, we thought we could help you out by doing our own investigation of Meranda's murder," announced Buzz.

The sheriff nodded his agreement.

"First, Macie and I checked out a suspect in Wayzata. That stranger who was reported to have been hanging around town the day before the body was found?" Buzz began.

"Yes, I wasn't able to figure out who that guy was."

"Well, we did. His name's Gary Anderson. He's a Wayzata resident who spent one night at the White House Hotel. Everything about the story he told Charlie at the hotel checked out perfectly in Wayzata. We talked with one of his neighbors and Anderson himself. He's not your guy, Sheriff."

"Good work, folks," the sheriff replied. "But please be careful in conducting your investigation. You're not trained law enforcement professionals like me, after all. These investigations can be dangerous."

"We're being careful, thanks. Macie and I then thought that we would go to St. Paul to check into Meranda's past. Given that she had recently been there, we thought that it was possible that someone from St. Paul might have murdered her. She had a run-in with a guy a few years back, but he has since moved to Duluth. After talking with several people there, we left without any additional suspects in St. Paul."

"I found a local suspect here that you should know about." Keith then related the story of Jerry, the ferry boat driver who had fallen for Meranda.

The Sheriff nodded adding, "Jerry? I know a lot of the boat drivers and they strike me as pretty good guys. But I'll definitely look into it. I'll have to find out just where he was that night."

The group left his office feeling hopeful that Keith might have found the murderer. In the meantime, their investigation would continue.

The next morning, Macie was preparing to leave the boarding house for work when someone knocked. It was Sheriff Herman again.

"Hello, Macie. Could you please stop by the jailhouse on your way to work? Given that you were the first to point out the potential billing fraud being committed by Vegas, I'd like to have you look at some of the additional evidence that I have collected from his cottage. We are preparing for his day in court."

"Sure, Sheriff. I'll stop by."

"Good. Thank you very much. See you soon."

A short time later, Macie walked into the jailhouse and found the sheriff in his office.

"Sit down, Macie, and let me show you some of the documents that I've collected."

Macie sifted through the documents, in some cases, comparing the figures in one document with those on another. "I would agree with you, Sheriff. You've collected additional evidence. These don't look like careless mistakes to me. It looks like he was intentionally overbilling multiple clients. The fraud was even more significant than we had originally estimated."

"Here's something unusual that I picked up in his place the morning that I arrested him. I wasn't sure what to make of it. Take a look."

Macie reached inside the box handed to her by the sheriff.

"A gold nugget!" she exclaimed. "My dad had one like this."

"Really!"

"Yes. In fact, this looks very similar to the one he had. But his was lost in the fire that killed my parents. However, I'm still struck by how similar this one appears to my father's. Doesn't the shape of this remind you a bit of a fish?"

"Yes, it does."

"They referred to my Dad's nugget as 'the Whale' because of its large size and its shape. I have a photo of my father holding his nugget. I'd be happy to get it to show you."

"Sure, let's take a look at your photo."

Macie left the office and returned 10 minutes later with her photo.

"Here you are, Sheriff."

The sheriff laid the photo next to the nugget.

"Well, I'll be! They do look a lot alike! Even the container holding the nugget looks similar," the sheriff exclaimed.

"Could this be my father's nugget? How could that be possible?" Macie wondered aloud.

"Let's go ask our prisoner a few questions," the sheriff proposed. "If you wouldn't mind coming with me, you can serve as a witness for this discussion."

Vegas glared as Macie and the sheriff approached his cell. She had never really paid that much attention to Vegas before, noting only that he seemed plain-spoken, reserved and almost anti-social. Now, Macie almost felt heat coming from his eyes. She shifted her focus away from his eyes to the thinning black hair slicked back on his head.

"Well if it ain't the bitch who's framing me!" scowled Vegas.

"Watch your language, Vegas, or your stay here in our jail might get much less comfortable. We have a couple of simple questions for you. You were in the process of packaging this nugget when I arrested you. Where did you get it?

"I bought it at a pawnshop in St. Louis," Vegas replied.

"What pawnshop?" the sheriff continued.

"I don't remember."

"Why did you lie when I asked you what you were packaging?"

"I didn't lie."

"Yes, you did. You said that you were packaging an agate to send back to St. Louis to add to your collection."

"I don't remember what I said."

"Vegas, I don't trust you as far as I could throw you. We're all going to rest easier when your ass ends up in the state penitentiary. We just need to gather our evidence to put you away."

"You won't find any valid evidence. I'm being framed. That bitch at your side is the likely criminal. She thinks she's clever in the way that she's framing me."

"Sorry, Macie. Let's leave this loser to ponder his long future in the pen." Vegas continued ranting from his cell as they closed the heavy jail door behind them.

The sheriff and Macie sat down again at his desk.

"I think we're finally seeing the real Vegas, Macie. It's amazing that he has been masquerading as a mild-mannered and competent lawyer for as long as he has. We've got to dig deeper into this situation. The nugget is a whole new topic that needs to be investigated."

"Sheriff, I think the answers surrounding that nugget can only be found in St. Louis. I would propose that I continue our investigation there. I think I need to review some of my early family history with my grandmother. She can provide me with more information about my father's nugget."

"If you can afford the time off from your work, Macie, I think your proposal makes sense. There are just too many coincidences here."

"I know that Mr. Jerome will let me take time off. I will see about taking the train to St. Louis as soon as I can."

Grandmother

After two days of train travel, Macie arrived in Florissant, Missouri, and headed straight to her grandmother's house where she knocked on the door.

The charming old woman beamed with pleasure at the sight of her granddaughter on her doorstep. "Macie, how glorious to see you! It's been far too long!" the woman exclaimed.

"Mmmmm", Macie purred as she reached out to give her grandmother a bear hug. "I'm sorry, Grandma. It HAS been far too long. We have so much to catch up on. I hope that you've been doing okay."

"Oh, you know. It's so hard to get old. My life is simple and unremarkable. Let's focus on you. Please fill me in on your adventures up there in Minnesota."

Her grandmother then led Macie

into her cozy living room where she seated herself in her rocking chair. Macie pulled up a chair, and, holding her grandmother's hand, began to describe her many adventures of the past weeks.

After an hour recounting tales related to her travels, her work, her new relationship, she shifted the topic of conversation.

"I've made some wonderful new friends, Grandma, in addition to Keith. My best friend turned out to be a very colorful older woman. She was incredibly kind to me and she was full of wisdom about life. She was bold and boisterous, and she made no effort to conform with social norms, but she was so comfortable with herself. I found her personality to be absolutely charming. We had so much fun together."

"I hear you referring to this friend of yours in the past tense. Why is that?" her grandmother inquired.

"Unfortunately, she died recently. The sheriff believes that she was murdered," Macie responded.

"Oh, dear!" the woman replied, a look of horror on her face. "Macie, that's awful. You're living in a very small, rural town, are you not? Things like that just don't happen."

"I know, Grandma," Macie replied. "It IS awful. One of my new friends works for the local newspaper. He and I are trying to help the sheriff to figure out what happened to our friend."

"If there is a murderer on the loose up there in your town in Minnesota, you could be in danger, Dear. I'm going to be worrying about you now," her grandmother replied.

"We're being careful, Grandma. Please don't worry about me," Macie answered. "But there's another story that I need to share with you and I'm hoping that you can help me with some additional information," Macie continued. "An attorney in Excelsior has recently been arrested. He's been defrauding several businesses up there. He's in jail now as he awaits a trial. Given that I was the one who uncovered the fraudulent activity, the sheriff asked me to assist him in identifying the evidence to use in the trial."

"It's impressive that the sheriff is relying on you to help with evidence."

"In the search we found a box that had been addressed to the attorney's home back here in St. Louis. You will not believe what we found in that box: a gold nugget that looks identical to the one that belonged to my father!!"

"What?! You don't think it's the actual nugget that belonged to your father, do you?"

"It sure looks like his nugget. It seems to have a similar shape. Even the tin container holding the nugget looks the same. Those photos of my parents and me that you sent me recently were very useful. As you probably recall, one of the photos showed my father holding his nugget. The sheriff and I compared the nugget found in the attorney's cottage to the photo and they appear to be identical. The attorney claims that he bought it at a pawnshop years ago here in St. Louis. I've forgotten the details of the story around that nugget. Could you please tell me again?"

"Sure. That nugget was mined in the Highlands near Butte, Montana, by your Uncle Roy. It was willed to your father by Roy. Your father took possession of it when Roy was killed in the mining accident. As I recall, it was the largest gold nugget ever found in the state of Montana.[27] It would be amazing if the nugget has shown up again."

"I agree. But it was clear to me that I needed to find out more about the nugget and the fire that killed my parents. You've gotten me off to a good start, Grandma. Could I stay here with you while I'm in St. Louis? I could sleep right here on your couch."

"Absolutely, Dear. It will be great to have you here," her grandmother replied, reaching out for another hug.

"I want to get started right away. First, I want to learn more about the fire. I'm going to visit the police department to see if they filed any reports about the fire," Macie continued.

"You might also want to read the newspaper articles about it," her grandmother added. "There were several articles about it, and I kept them. Could you please hand me that album over there on the shelf?"

Macie picked up the album and handed it to her grandmother who quickly located the relevant page. "Here, Dear. It makes me sad every time I look at these, but I understand why you feel compelled to learn more."

Macie began to read. The date of the newspaper had been handwritten onto the clipping: "June 8, 1878."

> *Florissant Farm Family Killed in Fire*
>
> *An early morning fire destroyed a St. Louis County farmhouse and killed John and Kathy Newman. The farmhouse had already been reduced to rubble by the time that firefighters arrived on the scene. The body of their 3-month-old daughter, Macie, has not yet been located. Authorities are investigating.*

"Then turn the page, Dear, as there is a second article about you."

This article was dated "June 10, 1878"

Girl Presumed Dead in Fire Found Alive

The 3-month-old daughter of John and Kathy Newman of Florissant who had been presumed dead in the fire that destroyed her family's home and killed her parents has been found alive. The child had been left unattended in the entryway of St. Mary's Girls Orphan Asylum in St. Louis. A note identifying the child was left in the basket next to her. There was no clue as to the identity of the person who had left the child there. The St. Louis police are investigating.

St. Mary's maintains and educates orphan and

homeless girls from age four to fourteen years. There are approximately 250 girls there at the present time.

A private party has expressed interest in adopting the child. The asylum is also checking with relatives of the child to explore other adoption possibilities.

"Do you recall if the police were ever able to locate the person who brought me to the orphanage?" Macie asked.

"I don't think so."

"Perhaps I should also go visit St. Mary's to see what they have in the way of records about my case."

"That sounds like a good idea and a good project for tomorrow. Meanwhile, you must be famished after all your travels. Let's rustle up some dinner and get you a good night's sleep."

"That sounds ideal, Grandma. It's so nice to be able to spend some time with you."

St. Mary's

Macie was up early the next morning and walked to the train station to catch the first trolley to downtown St. Louis. After a 45-minute ride, she got off at Olive and Grand and transferred to another trolley continuing along Olive until reaching 14th street. There she stepped down and finished the last few blocks on foot.

Macie was contemplative as she turned onto Biddle Street. As she approached a large, nondescript red brick building on the right, she spotted the sign:

> St. Mary's Girls' Orphan Asylum,
> Established 1843
> Serving Girls from Age 4 to 14[28]

She approached the entryway of the orphanage then paused to contemplate the place where she had been left as a baby.

Entering the building, she approached the receptionist at the desk as muffled sounds of large numbers of girls in back rooms resonated through the lobby. "Can I help you," the woman inquired.

"Hello. My name is Macie Stewart and my adoption was handled by this institution back in 1878. I would be interested in seeing any records that you have about my stay here and my adoption."

"Perhaps our director, Mrs. Perkins, can help you. Just a moment, please." She got up and knocked on the door of a nearby office and then looked inside. "There's a Macie Stewart here who would like to see you. She was a resident here about 20 years ago and is seeking records about her case."

"I'll be right out," Mrs. Perkins replied.

Mrs. Perkins, a bespectacled and professional-looking woman soon appeared and walked up to Macie, reaching out to shake her hand.

"Hello, Macie. It's very nice to meet you," Mrs. Perkins said, smiling broadly. "What can I do for you?"

"I was abandoned on your doorstep back in 1878 when I was a baby. My parents had been killed in a housefire. I believe that your organization handled my adoption. I would like to learn as much as I can about my time here."

"Ah, yes. I actually remember your case as it was unusual in many respects. I think that we're going to be able to help you with some details about your short stay with us. Please come into my office and have a seat," she said, closing the door behind her. "Before we look back in our records, would you mind giving me a quick update on your life after you left us?"

"Of course," Macie replied and started recounting a few key details about her upbringing, schooling, her employment with Mr. Jerome, and her current summer in Excelsior. Macie avoided any mention of Meranda's murder or the investigation into the nugget. Instead, she framed her current interest in the adoption records as part of a genealogical effort.

"That is fascinating. Thank you very much for the update. We rarely get an opportunity to hear first-hand accounts about life after St. Mary's." Mrs. Perkins stood up and walked toward a wall of file cabinets.

"I do remember some things about your case. It was sad to learn of the loss of your parents in the fire. And to think that the beautiful baby that you were somehow ended up on our doorstep after such a tragedy ... it is not the kind of thing that any of us who were here at the time will ever forget." Mrs. Perkins continued shuffling through files. "What year was that again?"

"It was 1878," Macie replied.

Mrs. Perkins pulled a file folder from one of the drawers and looked it over. "Here we are. Would you like me to read our case notes to you or would you like to look them over yourself?"

"I'd love to look them over. I brought some paper with me and I would like to carefully document everything that you have."

"Sure," she said, handing the documents to Macie. "I can't let them be taken out of my office, but you're welcome to sit at the desk there while you review them. I have a lot of work to do while you review but please don't hesitate if questions come to mind."

"Thank you very much," Macie replied as she began to skim the documents.

There were several sheets of paper with entries by date. The first entry dated June 9, 1878, 7:30 a.m., described her arrival at the orphanage. It listed the items that were found with her. A note left in the basket read: "This is Macie Newman from Florissant. Her parents were killed in a housefire. Please take good care of her."

Macie sighed and paused, trying to envision the person who had written this note and trying to imagine how that person had been involved in the whole affair. She resumed reading. The orphanage notes then indicated that the police were contacted and would be over shortly to investigate. Notes indicated that the baby was moved into the nursery while efforts were undertaken to locate relatives.

"Excuse me, Mrs. Perkins. Do you recall if the police were ever able to figure out anything about the person who brought me here?"

"I don't believe they were ever able to learn a thing about that person."

The next document was also dated June 9, 1878. The time cited was 3:30 p.m. It mentioned that the orphanage was visited by Mr. and Mrs. Stewart. Macie gasped inwardly at this reference to her adoptive parents. She quickly continued reading. The notes mentioned in parentheses that Mr. Stewart is the prominent St. Louis real estate magnate. According to the notes, the couple had expressed interest in adopting a child, preferably a baby girl. The Stewarts were then informed that, by chance, a baby girl had just arrived at the facility. It was too early to say as to whether that child might be available for adoption, pending contact with potential relatives of the family. They were also told that they might be able to provide temporary care for the child while permanent arrangements were being explored. The Stewarts mentioned that they had a nursery in their home already fully equipped as they had been attempting to have their own child for some time.

Macie looked up from her reading. "Excuse me again, Mrs. Perkins. Another question for you, please. How common is it or has it been for babies to be abandoned on your entryway?"

Mrs. Perkins replied, "It does happen but it's rare."

"And how common is it for people to come here asking about adopting a baby girl?"

"Most people who visit us to inquire about children who might be adopted realize that we deal primarily with older children. It would be rare that people would come to us in search of a baby," Mrs. Perkins replied.

"Does it strike you as unusual that my adoptive parents visited your facility and asked specifically about adopting a baby girl on the very afternoon that I was left here?" Macie probed.

"Hmmm ... I had not thought

about that but, I would say that, yes, that does seem pretty coincidental," Mrs. Perkins replied.

Macie jotted down some notes and then resumed reading.

The next entry was dated June 10, 1878. It was determined that baby Macie Newman was the daughter of the St. Louis County couple who had just been killed in a fire. A copy of the *St. Louis Post-Dispatch* newspaper article was attached.

The following document caught Macie by complete surprise. It was a short letter dated July 2, 1878. It read:

> *My wife and I have been offered the opportunity to adopt our granddaughter, Macie Newman. While we would love to be able to adopt her into our family, our poor health and our limited financial means force us to decline. Furthermore, we feel that Macie will be*

> *better off being adopted by Mr. and Mrs. Stewart who have been providing care for Macie over the past month.*

The letter was signed by Oliver Newman, Macie's paternal grandfather.

The next document was a similar letter, dated July 6th, this one signed by her maternal grandfather.

> *We would love to be able to adopt our granddaughter, Macie. I am very sick. My wife has big troubles in caring for me alone. We hardly have money to survive. Macie will do better with Mr. and Mrs. Stewart. They are rich and will do right by her.*

Macie sighed and clasped her head in her hands as tears filled her eyes. She had never heard that her grandparents had been approached about adopting her. After a minute, she wiped away the tears and continued reading.

The final document[29] contained the following entry:

> *From the Office of the Recorder of Deeds, St. Louis County, Missouri:*
>
> *Newman, Macie G., a female child born on February 22, 1878, in St. Louis County, Missouri, abandoned to St. Mary's Girls' Orphan Asylum of St. Louis County. Adopted by Donald & Melanie Stewart of St. Louis who have had said child for 90 days. Name of said child to be known as Macie G. Stewart. Recorded September 23, 1878, in Warranty Deed Book 49, Page 19.*

Macie closed the file and closed her eyes, deep in thought. She then reopened the file, returned to the first page, and began writing more notes in earnest.

After scribbling furiously for 30 minutes or so, she closed the file again while keeping one document in her hand. "Excuse me again, Mrs. Perkins. I have one more question for you, please. Can you help me with this last document," Macie inquired, referring her to the warranty deed.

"Sure. Since approximately the 1850s, adoptions in our state are done by filing a deed with the County Court. That's the way that your adoption was documented in the Warranty Deed book of the county where your adoptive parents resided."

"Ahh. Thank you very much for the tremendous help you've given me today. I've learned so much about my past! I now have some new questions for my grandmother," handing the folder back to Mrs. Perkins. "But first I'd like to visit the police headquarters. Can you please tell me where that is located?"

"You're in luck! It's not far at all. Go west along Biddle for about six blocks. Go north on North 16th Street a block to O'Fallon Street and you'll see the building to your left."

"Sounds good. Thanks again."

"It's been very nice to meet you, Macie," Mrs. Perkins replied as she rose to escort Macie out of the building. "Please do not hesitate to call on me again if I can be of further assistance." They shook hands and Macie headed for the police headquarters.

Macie stepped up to the desk of the young man in police uniform, the third desk she had visited this afternoon as people kept referring her to their colleagues. Her hopes of finding useful information were starting to dim as the facility was giving her the impression of one that was not very efficient or well-organized. "Hopefully, this man will be more helpful," she thought to herself.

"Just a moment, Ma'am," the officer said, not even lifting his head to look at Macie while he continued to write. Finally, he set his pen down and looked up. "Sorry to keep you waiting, Ma'am. I'm Officer Betchwars," shaking Macie's hand. "Can I help you?"

She introduced herself and told the officer about the Florissant housefire in 1878 that killed her parents and her abandonment on the steps of St. Mary's. He jotted down some notes as she spoke. "I would like to find out if your staff was ever able to learn anything about the cause of the housefire or the person who left me at St. Mary's."

"Well you are talking to the right person here. I'm in charge of our archives. But your case was way before my time so I have no idea what we might have back there for you. It'll take us a while, probably a couple of hours, to see what we have."

"Thank you, sir. I'll wait."

"There's a little lounge down that hall on the left where you can wait. If you're lucky, you might find some coffee there although it's typically on the stale side."

"Thank you again. I'll wait there."

"All right. I'll come get you as soon as we figure out what we've got."

About three hours later, the officer stepped into the lounge. "Miss Stewart," he said as he approached Macie, "if you'll come with me, I'll show you what we have."

They returned to his desk where a large box awaited them. "Unfortunately, we don't have much that is likely to be very helpful to you. We've still got the basket and the blankets in which you were left at the asylum," lifting the items from the box and setting them on his desk.

Macie fought back the tears that were forming in her eyes.

"We've also got a couple of reports in here. The first one describes interviews with St. Mary's employees. Apparently, none of them saw anything suspicious that morning, except for the receptionist who found you on the steps when she reported for her shift. Here's the note that was attached to the basket," placing it in front of Macie for her to review.

Macie reviewed the note and confirmed that St. Mary's copy of it was correct.

He continued. "Another officer

had contacted the sheriff in Florissant to see if they had any leads after investigating the housefire. Apparently, they didn't find anything that might explain the cause of the fire. They also had no idea on how you ended up surviving it. I can let you look at the report if you like."

"Yes, I would like to see it." She read for a minute then looked up again.

"I'm sorry, Miss Stewart," he continued, "but yours is definitely in the cold case category."

"Well, I'm doing some investigation on my own here in St. Louis. I've already learned some things of interest this morning over at St. Mary's."

"Please come back to see me if you uncover anything that could help us to close up this cold case once and for all."

"I will definitely do so. Thank you very much, Officer Betchwars."

With that, Macie headed for her grandma's.

Questions

"It was an extremely interesting morning at St. Mary's, Grandma. I learned more than I could have expected or hoped. Some of it was a bit painful." Macie pulled up a chair on the right side of her grandma's rocking chair, the side with her "good" ear.

"Tell me about it, Dear," her grandma replied, grabbing hold of Macie's hands.

"They had a letter from you and grandfather in which you said that you could not afford to adopt me," her voice faltering and a tear streaming down her cheek.

"Oh, dear. We never thought that you would ever see that letter. Yes, we were asked about adopting you, but those times were so hard! Your grandfather was already very ill. We were barely managing to survive as it was."

Macie's tears continued. "Please tell me everything, Grandma."

"I hate to admit this, but your adoptive father also gave us a financial incentive to submit that letter."

"He paid you to give me up?"

"Essentially, that's true. I'm very sorry, Dear. Please forgive me," she added, her eyes welling with tears. She reached out to Macie to give her a hug.

"It's okay, Grandma. I understand. I forgive you. So, did my stepfather come to meet with you?"

"Yes, he did. Both he and your stepmother came to visit us. They brought you along with them too. They were a very nice couple. It was clear to us that you would be well cared for with them."

"So, did you write the letter then and there?"

"No, they had their attorney come to visit us a few days later. He told us what to say in the letter and he gave us the payment. I still remember that fellow. He had an unusual name: Vegas."

"I don't suppose that you mean Vegas Thorpe?"

"Yes, I do believe that was his name. Why? Do you know him?"

"I can't believe this. Yes, I do know him. He is part of the reason that I'm here. He is the lawyer who is now in jail back in Excelsior! I had no idea that he had worked for my stepfather. I'm surprised that Mr. Jerome, the man I'm working for, has never mentioned it to me. On the other hand, I know that Vegas used to work for Mr. Jerome but left to go off on his own many years ago. Perhaps Mr. Jerome forgot."

"I'm glad that you're finding this helpful."

"This is incredibly helpful, Grandma. I have other questions for you too. Do you have any idea how my stepparents found out about me? It's almost as if they knew that I was available for adoption."

"Actually, I think I do. Your father did some gardening for the Stewarts. And they had an annual picnic for their staff and the families of their staff. I'm pretty sure that that's how your stepparents would've learned about you."

"Interesting! Just a second, Grandma. I've got to jot down some of these things in my notes." Macie scribbled furiously as she started to put two and two together then resumed her questioning.

"Back to this photo of Dad again with the nugget." Macie handed the photo of her father with the golden nugget to her grandma.

"Yes?"

"Do you think there's a chance that my father would have sold the nugget?"

"I really don't think so. While times were hard for everyone and the nugget could've been sold for a lot of money, that nugget also had great sentimental value to your father as a link to his brother."

"You can see now why I'm trying to piece all of this together. I've got to jot down a few more notes then set all this aside for a while. I'll sleep on this tonight. Hopefully, with a fresh brain tomorrow, I'll be able to make some sense of it all."

"I have some leftover pot roast in the icebox. We can cook up some potatoes and carrots. How about dinner?"

"That would be wonderful, Grandma. I'm famished!"

Zunker Photography

Macie was restless during the night trying to make sense of all that she had learned. She finally got up, lit a lantern and picked up her notes. She shuffled through the papers looking briefly at each one. Her thoughts turned to the timeline of events.

"I was born on February 22 and the fire occurred on June 7th when I was about 3 months old." She turned to the photo of her parents holding her as a baby. "I must have been pretty close to that age when the photo was taken. I wonder if it would be helpful to find out exactly when the photo was taken. The gold nugget would still have been in my father's possession through that date." Her attention turned to the edge of the frame around the photo where the name of the photographer appeared: T. J. Zunker Photography.

"Perhaps the photographer would have records showing when the photo was taken."

She continued reviewing documents in search of new questions as the sun started to peek into the house.

"Good morning, Dear," her grandmother called as she entered the room. "I hope that you slept well."

"I did sleep well for most of the night. However, I've got new questions on my mind. Do you know where T. J. Zunker Photography is located?"

"Yes, I believe they're in Bridgeton. I'm pretty sure that they're still in business."

"And how about a jeweler? Can you think of one in the area? I have a new question about the nugget with which a jeweler could probably help."

"I think Mr. James, the owner of the general store in Bridgeton does some jewelry work on the side. If I'm thinking of the right person, I've heard he's very skilled at it."

"Wonderful! Do you think one of your neighbors could take me over to Bridgeton?"

"I suspect that Mr. Green next door would be happy to do so. He's always offering me assistance. Let's have a bite to eat. It's a bit too early to tap on his door."

They headed for the kitchen, arm in arm.

Later that morning Mr. Green and Macie pulled up to the house in which Zunker Photography was apparently located. "I'll just sit out here to wait for you," Mr. Green said, as he stepped down from the wagon then offered his hand to help Macie.

"Thanks, Mr. Green. This shouldn't take very long."

Macie knocked on the door and a young man appeared.

"Hello, Miss. What can I do for you? Would you like to step in?"

"Sure. Thank you. I'm Macie Stewart although I was born Macie Newman. I was born in Florissant and I'm curious about a photograph that someone from your studio took of my family when I was a baby." Macie pulled out the photo and handed it to the man.

"This photo would have been taken by my father. He passed away about two years ago. I'm not sure how much I can tell you about the photo."

"Is there any chance that your father kept records of the photographs that he took? My question really relates to when the photo was taken."

"In that case, perhaps I'll be able to help you. My father was extremely detailed and somewhat of a packrat. We still have all his appointment books. In what year do you think this was taken?"

"In the spring of 1878."

"Why don't you have a seat here and give me a few minutes while I see what I can find."

Macie sat down while the young man disappeared into a back room. He emerged soon carrying a small book.

"We're in luck! Here's his appointment book for the years from 1878 to 1881." He flipped forward in the book until he stopped and scanned one page. "Here we are: Newman family, Florissant, 1 p.m. Your family had a reservation with him on June 5th, 1878."

Macie added some new notes to herself.

"If you don't mind, I'm curious as to why you are so interested in the date of the photograph," the man inquired.

"I've returned to St. Louis to learn as much as I can about my earliest childhood. This photo is a treasured keepsake and I was curious as to when it was taken."

"I see. Is there anything else that I can do for you?" the man inquired.

"Actually, there is one more favor I would like to ask. Could you please create a little note detailing what we have just learned? It could say: 'The two family photographs shown to me today by Macie Newman Stewart including the one of her father holding his golden nugget were taken by my father, Thomas Zunker, on June 5th, 1878.' If you could sign and date that note with your studio name, that would be great."

"That sounds like we're creating a document for use in a court trial."

"It is possible that it might be. I'd like to be prepared just in case."

"Sure, I'm happy to help," he said, as he took a sheet of paper and began writing.

"You've been extremely helpful.

Thank you very much," she said, as he handed her the paper.

"You're very welcome, Miss."

Macie arose as the man opened the door and ushered her out.

"That went very well, Mr. Green. Could you please give me just a few more minutes while I walk down to the general store to ask a few questions?"

"Sure, Miss Macie. Take your time. I have nothing pressing to do today."

"Thank you. This shouldn't take long."

Macie soon reached the store and walked in. Mr. James was finishing up with another patron.

"Can I help you, Miss?"

"You are Mr. James?" Macie inquired.

"I am. What can I do for you?"

"I understand that you do some work with jewelry."

"That I do. It's actually my passion."

"I have a couple of questions with which I'm hoping you can help me. I'm curious about this golden nugget that was owned by my father." Macie handed the photo to him.

"That is one incredible nugget!" he exclaimed.

"It was one of the largest ever found in the state of Montana," Macie noted.

"What would you like to know?"

"I'm curious about what would happen to it in a housefire. Would it melt?"

"No, it would not melt in the typical housefire. The melting point of gold is much higher than the temperature at which a housefire would likely burn. Now as for that container holding the nugget -- that looks like tin to me. If true, that container would likely melt in the fire as tin has a fairly low melting point."

"That's all I need to know, Mr.

James. Thank you very much."

"Do you know the weight of that nugget?" he asked.

"Oh, good question! No, I don't."

"The value of the nugget will be directly related to its weight. The weight of gold is measured in troy ounces."

"Troy ounces?"

"Yes, I'll spare you the complex details. But gold can be weighed in a traditional fashion in ounces then converted to troy ounces by dividing the value by 1.097."

"That's very interesting, Mr. James. I need to capture that." She paused to write down the formula then continued. "I will definitely find out about the weight of the nugget."

"If you would ever like to do something with that nugget, please come on back. There are a lot of interesting things that could be done with it. I could also help you sell it. It would likely be worth a substantial sum."

"I'll keep that in mind. Thank you again." Macie left the store and returned to Mr. Green in his wagon.

"Success!" Macie reported as she took Mr. Green's hand and climbed up into the wagon.

"I'm glad to hear it," Mr. Green replied as he climbed aboard and sat down next to Macie. "I'd love to hear about your visits if you'd care to share." With a "Giddy-up" and a light flick on the reins, the wagon was off on its return trip to Florissant.

Puzzles

"While you were out, Dear, a telegram arrived for you," her grandma said, handing the message to Macie.

"It's from Keith!" Macie's heart began to race as she read silently. "My darling Macie. Missing you tremendously! Be safe and come home soon! Love, Keith." She then repeated the message aloud for her grandma.

"Ah, that's sweet! He sounds like a fine young man, Dear."

"He is Grandma. You'll love him. I miss him dearly.

"He's got to be a wonderful young man if he is good enough for my Macie!" They beamed at each other.

"Grandma, my visit to the jeweler raised an interesting new question. Did my Dad or Uncle Roy ever tell you the weight of the nugget?"

"Yes, I believe that your uncle mentioned it in the letter that he wrote after he found the nugget."

"Do you still have that letter?"

"I'm pretty sure that I do. It'll take me a bit to put my hands on it, but I will certainly try to find it."

"Thanks! There is just one more thing that I would like to explore while I'm here, Grandma. Can you think of anyone who would have worked for my stepfather at the time that my dad was doing the gardening for him? Someone who would also have been at one of those employee picnics?"

"Yes, I believe that Mr. Jones down the street did a variety of carpentry work for him. He would likely have been invited to the picnics. He's about two blocks down on the right side of the street. There's a huge willow in front of his house."

"I'm on my way, Grandma.

Thanks!" Macie said as she left the house.

She could see the willow from the street in front of her grandmother's house. Soon she was there and knocked on the door.

An elderly gentleman answered.

"Mr. Jones?"

"Yup! What can I do for you, Miss?"

"I'm Macie Stewart. I'm the daughter of John and Kathy Newman. My father did some gardening for Mr. Stewart before he was killed in that housefire."

"You're Newman's daughter? I remember your father well. He was a great guy. That was an incredible tragedy, that housefire. Would you like to sit down?" motioning to chairs on his porch.

"No thanks. This should not take long and I'm in a bit of a hurry. I understand that you did some carpentry work for Mr. Stewart. True?"

"That's correct, Miss. I still do some work for him on occasion. He has developed many large homes in this area and there's always plenty of carpentry work to be done. Some of that work comes my way."

"I've been told that Mr. Stewart held annual picnics for his staff. Is that correct?"

"He did indeed – at least years ago. He doesn't seem to care as much about relations with his staff these days. There hasn't been a picnic for maybe 15 years or so."

"Did Mr. Stewart typically spend time with all of you at the picnic?"

"Not really. He would usually show up to say a few words to the group. Then he would walk around, quickly greet everyone, and head back into his house while we ate. He always seemed in a hurry to exit the scene."

"Did Mrs. Stewart participate in the picnics?"

"Yes, she usually did and she was

quite sociable. She mingled at length with all of us. She was always especially fond of the children, particularly the babies. I will never forget her holding our twin boys at the same time when they were babies -- one in each arm! She often mentioned how much she would like to have a child of her own."

"That doesn't surprise me. The Stewarts adopted me after the fire. She was a wonderful mother to me."

"I vaguely recall that they had adopted a child."

"Do you recall if the picnic was held at the same time each year?"

"Yes, it was. It was always held on the Sunday before Memorial Day."

"I think that's all I need to know for now. Thank you very much, Mr. Jones."

"Don't hesitate to contact me again if any other questions come to mind. I'm sorry again about the loss of your parents. They were truly fine people. It had to be an act of God that you somehow survived."

"I'm trying to figure some things out on exactly that point. Your information helps enormously. Thank you again." She turned and walked away.

Her grandma met her at the door when Macie returned.

"Good news," her grandmother reported. "Here's the letter," she said, handing it to Macie. "The nugget weighed 27.5 troy ounces."

Macie quickly scanned the letter which gave all kinds of details about the finding of the nugget.

"Could I please borrow this letter, Grandma? This is a critical document!"

"Absolutely, Dear. What a day you've had. I've got some dinner just about ready for you." They then headed for the kitchen.

Later that evening, Macie took out her notes again and tried to piece all the new information together into a cohesive story in her mind. "My adoptive parents most likely meet baby me at the picnic in late-May...My family is photographed a few days later and only two days before the fire...The fire occurs...The newspaper reports the fire and our deaths...I'm left at the orphanage...My adoptive parents show up and take me to their home...The next day the newspaper reports that I have been found alive and left at the orphanage...My adoptive parents are at the orphanage before the newspaper report of my survival..."

Suddenly Macie exclaimed aloud: "How could that be?! Is it a coincidence that they showed up when they did in search of a baby girl?!"

Her thoughts continued. "My grandparents are paid off in exchange for passing on the opportunity to adopt me...My adoptive mother always stressed how much she had wanted to have a child...It was clearly a source of friction in their marriage that they could not have a child...Could my adoptive father, God forbid, have had something to do with the housefire? The nugget, still in the possession of my family at the time of the fire, shows up in Excelsior 20 years later in the possession of Vegas Thorpe. Could Vegas, my adoptive father's attorney at the time, been involved in that fire? The evidence seemed to suggest that all of this was likely."

Tears filled her eyes as she pondered the gravity of her conclusions.

The following morning Macie was ready to wish her grandma goodbye and return to Excelsior.

"Macie, Dear. Aren't you going to visit your stepfather while you're here?"

"No, Grandma. I really don't think he cares that much about me. If my stepmother were still alive, I'd be there. I miss her dearly! Furthermore, there are some things that I've found through my investigation here this week that I find troubling about my stepfather and the way I ended up in his care. So, no, I'm not going to visit him."

"Macie, I hope you know how proud your parents would be of the wonderful young woman you have become."

"Thank you, Grandma. How I wish that I could have known them!"

"And I'm so happy for you and your exciting new relationship with Keith. Are those wedding bells that I hear?"

"Ah, Grandma. We're not there yet. But I feel so lucky to have Keith in my life. You'll adore him."

"Let's hope I live long enough to meet him."

"I'll definitely bring him along next time I come to visit. Or maybe you could come visit us in Excelsior!"

"Oh, I don't think I'm up to traveling anymore. I'm just too old. Well, Macie, I hate to say 'goodbye' but if you're going to catch your train today, you'd better be on your way. Come here, you darling thing," enveloping her in a bear hug.

"Goodbye, Grandma. Thank you for everything!" and Macie was out the door, turning once more to wave from the street.

Searching Anew

"Hello, Macie. Welcome back!" Buzz arose from his desk at the *Journal* and reached out to give Macie a hug.

"It's great to see you, Buzz."

"I can't wait to hear about your trip."

"I've got so much to tell you. We might as well head straight to the sheriff's office so I can recount my story to both of you at the same time."

"All right, let's go."

As Macie and Buzz headed up the boardwalk along Water Street, Buzz commented. "While I've got a little opportunity, I've been waiting to tell you something."

"What's up, Buzz?"

"Remember that discussion about my wife going to work?"

"Sure."

"My thinking has just come around. I'm ready to tell my wife that I will support her decision to get involved in animal care again. That part-time position is still open. I'm also ready to take on some new responsibilities around our home."

"Your wife will be thrilled, Buzz. Don't you have an anniversary coming up soon?"

"Yes, our 25th, next week. Why?"

"What about sharing all of this as part of an anniversary present? I guarantee that your wife will be very touched."

"Macie, you are too much! What a wonderful idea! Thank you!"

They arrived at the brick building that housed the sheriff's office and the jail and entered. The sheriff was sipping coffee with his feet up on his desk. He quickly stood up.

"Welcome home, Macie. I hope that your trip to St. Louis was informative."

"It certainly was. You had both better sit down as I've got a lot to share with you."

"First, I've got some information for you, Macie. I took the suggestion that you sent via telegram and had the jeweler in Wayzata weigh the nugget: 27.5 troy ounces."

"Wow! That's the exact same weight cited by my uncle in a letter to my grandparents when he found the nugget. It's pretty obvious that we have THE nugget that had belonged to my father."

Macie then carefully and completely recounted all the insights that she had gathered about that tumultuous series of events back in Florissant and St. Louis in 1878. She also showed them the evidence which she had brought back.

"The bottom line, Sheriff, if I am correct that Vegas was involved in the housefire that killed my parents, I think it is also possible that he killed Meranda."

"That's a stunning thought!" the sheriff replied.

Macie continued: "Let's think for a second. Vegas was packaging the nugget on the morning that Meranda's body was found. Do we think that was just a coincidence?"

"Hmmm...perhaps not."

"Vegas lied when you asked what he was packaging?"

"Correct. He did, that bastard."

"Doesn't that suggest that he's hiding something – probably something important?"

"Probably so."

"Here's another thing that occurred to me on my way back from St. Louis thinking through all of this. I showed the photo of my father with his golden nugget to only two people in Excelsior: to Keith and to Meranda. Meranda was very captivated with that photo. My hunch is that Meranda visited Vegas' cottage on the night of the murder. If you recall she and Vegas had had a good time dancing together at the ball. My hunch is that she saw the golden nugget in his cottage. I suspect that she could not contain her shock on seeing it. She likely blurted out the fact that she recognized it and knew who it had belonged to. Upon challenging Vegas about it, Vegas knew that it could tie him to the murder of my parents."

"So Vegas killed her right there and then to guard his secret?" Buzz surmised.

"That's exactly what I'm suggesting. After killing Meranda, he was packaging the nugget, intending to get it out of town – fast! Fortunately, he didn't have a chance to send it because that was the morning that you arrested him."

"Well I'll be! It does sound possible. Amazing legwork, Macie! We'll have to take another look inside his cottage -- this time for evidence of murder!"

"Vegas is still locked up?" Macie inquired.

"He certainly is. On the morning that I visited him for the potentially fraudulent billing that you uncovered, he was drunk as a skunk. So, I placed him under arrest. He also resisted. He got off a punch to my chin although he was too drunk to really ding me. He had already spent a night in jail and paid a fine earlier this summer for drinking. I had warned him that if he forgot again that Excelsior is dry, his ass would end up in my jail for a good spell next time. So that's where he sits today as he awaits his trial."[30]

"Good. That's where he belongs," Macie replied.

"So far, he's looking at charges for billing fraud, intoxication and assault. I'd like the two of you to accompany me on a new search of his cottage. You have clearly outdone me in investigating your friend's murder. I should get a new search warrant. Could you meet me this afternoon, say 3:00?"

Macie turned to Buzz who was shaking his head. "We'll be back here at 3:00 sheriff."

Shortly after 3:00, Macie, Buzz and the sheriff entered Vegas's cottage.

The discovery was almost immediate. "Sheriff!" cried Macie. "There! On the back side of the coat rack. It's Meranda's scarf! And look," she said, pointing to the scarf, "here's the cross pin given to her by the church ladies just before she went to St. Paul!"

"Well, I'll be! I guess I can't fault myself for not noticing that. I was focused on finding evidence for fraud in the form of paperwork."

After looking around the cottage for a while and not finding anything else seemingly related to Meranda or the murder, the sheriff suggested a halt to the search. "That scarf alone is huge. We've got some new questions to ask of our prisoner. Why don't you come with me to witness the interrogation?"

They quickly returned to the jail.

"Vegas, we've got a few simple questions for you," said the sheriff as Vegas approached the bars on his cell.

"Yeah, what do you want to know this time? I see you brought that bitch who's been framing me back again."

"Did you know Meranda Delaquila?"

"Sure," Vegas replied. "I think just about everyone in town knew her. She and I even danced a bit at the St. Louis Hotel ball. But I can't say that I knew her very well."

"Did she ever visit you at your cottage?"

"Nope."

"Then would you care to explain how her scarf was found on the coatrack inside your cottage?"

"She's framing me again," pointing at Macie. "Meranda never set foot in my cottage. I'm done talking. I want my attorney."

Clippings

From the *Excelsior Journal*, January 19, 1900:

*Local Attorney Guilty of Murder
by Buzz Greenfield*

The jury in the Meranda Delaquila murder trial needed three days of deliberations before finding attorney Vegas Thorpe guilty of first-degree murder. Thorpe was found guilty of murdering the Excelsior summer visitor in his cottage on the evening of August 1st, 1899. The prosecution proved that Mrs. Delaquila was murdered when she discovered evidence linking Thorpe to an unsolved murder in the St. Louis, Missouri, area 22 years prior.

Before the sentencing proceedings began, prosecuting attorney Mr. Joseph Green, made an offer to Thorpe which he has accepted. In exchange for Thorpe's agreement to testify for the prosecution in a separate trial for that unsolved St. Louis murder, Thorpe might be offered a reduced sentence. The actual sentencing for Thorpe will be delayed until after his appearance and testimony in that trial in St. Louis.

From the *Excelsior Journal*, August 10, 1900:

*Convicted Local Attorney Sentenced
by Buzz Greenfield*

Vegas Thorpe, who was convicted in January of murdering local summer resident Meranda Delaquila, was sentenced to 18 years in the state penitentiary. The sentence imposed upon Thorpe was reduced after Thorpe testified and provided evidence for the prosecution in a separate case against his former employer, a prominent St. Louis real estate developer, Donald Stewart. In that trial, Stewart was found guilty of ordering the murder of a Florissant, Missouri, farm family in a housefire in 1878. That fire killed the biological parents of Stewart's adopted daughter, Macie Stewart (born Macie Newman), who has been living in Excelsior since last summer and working at the St. Louis Hotel for Mr. Will Jerome. Developer Stewart was sentenced to 20 years in the Missouri State Penitentiary.

Blooming

At last, the big day arrived for Macie and Keith. It was a lovely afternoon, the 16th of June 1901, the lake sparkling in the sun, sailboats, motorboats and ferry boats active in every bay.

Inside the church, an eager crowd of guests waited anxiously for the bride's appearance. Final preparations were taking place in a side room behind the scenes. "Hold still, Macie," Mrs. O. requested in buttoning the wedding gown. Mrs. O. had volunteered her skills as expert seamstress to create the beautiful gown based on ideas from Macie and her new girlfriends. The result? "Stunning," they all agreed, especially the bride who exclaimed "It's divine, Mrs. O." The dress, of brilliant white satin, curved closely around Macie's slim figure and featured a very full skirt over several petticoats with a short train and a modest fitted bodice with lace trim.

When music signaled the start of the ceremony, an usher walked to the altar and placed two items there in a prominent spot for all to see: a photo of a young couple holding a baby and a lavender blue scarf. Everyone in attendance then focused on the aisle where an usher was leading Keith's grandparents to their seats. Keith then entered the sanctuary escorting his mother, followed by his father. After embracing them, Keith returned to the back of the sanctuary, this time to escort Macie's grandmother, just arrived by train from St. Louis, and wearing a lovely blue tulle gown. Next Keith took his place at the altar. Everyone held their breaths as the beautiful bride entered on the arm of her longtime friend and employer, the distinguished Sir Will Jerome, looking more dapper than ever, wearing a tuxedo. As Macie reached her handsome bridegroom at the altar, her grandmother stepped up, gave Macie a brief hug, then proudly reached out for the bridal bouquet, a role traditionally handled by the maid of honor. As Macie turned again to face her husband-to-be, Keith whispered quietly, "Hello, gorgeous! I love you. I'm the luckiest man alive to be marrying you!" Following a brief spiritual ceremony, ending with the traditional kiss, the couple turned together to face the congregation, expressing their approval and joy with enthusiastic applause. The newlyweds, beaming, strolled down the aisle hand in hand, first steps in their marital journey together.

Celebrating

Bugles blew, trumpets blared and a large chartered steamer pulled up to the dock carrying a crowd of laughing, excited people arriving directly from the Duggan wedding. The day had finally arrived for the dry run of the opening of the Big Island Amusement Park. This wedding reception was to be the THE social event of the summer. Excelsior, Deephaven, Wayzata and Minneapolis friends of the bride and groom were breathlessly anticipating their first experience in this much-awaited amusement park.

As the guests started to disembark from the steamer, the lone eagle who lived at the top of the island's most barren tree, took off and, in a seemingly welcoming gesture, flew low over the wedding party.

For Thomas Louden, Will Jerome and Keith Duggan as developers and architect, it was the culmination of their planning, designing and building this unique island park, in a natural rare setting surrounded by one of the largest lakes in Minnesota. The three men were jubilant as they watched their group of happy folks discover the pleasures of this new park. The joy radiating from this group made the three confident that the park would attract hordes of regular guests starting with the official grand opening the next day.

Mr. Jerome, surrounded by his wife and family, friends and admirers, said to his architect friend, "Keith, I don't know of any other project I've been involved in that I enjoyed more than this. This is a wonderful place for people and their families, not the upper crust. You and your team did a fabulous job."

Keith, with his beaming new bride, Macie, at his side, expressed his appreciation to Mr. Jerome and Mr. Louden for their remarkable investments and faith in the project. Then, turning to Macie, he exclaimed, "Now, let's go hear the music." All the wedding guests followed behind the newlyweds as they made their way along the manicured walkway to the music pavilion. The orchestra was already playing a beautiful and familiar piece as the group arrived. A soloist was singing.

> *My wild Irish Rose, the sweetest flower that grows.*
> *You may search everywhere, but none can compare with my wild Irish Rose.*
> *My wild Irish Rose, the dearest flower that grows,*
> *And some day for my sake, she may let me take the bloom from my wild Irish Rose.*

The group made its way to the side of the dance floor where a large section of seating was set up and decorated lavishly with orchids.

Once the entire party had arrived, Mr. Jerome and Thomas Louden of the TCRT stepped to the microphone on the stage. The music stopped. After a brief pause, Thomas Louden addressed the crowd.

"Good evening, ladies and gentlemen. Welcome to Big Island Park! I am Thomas Louden, founder of Twin City Rapid Transit and the primary investor in this park. We hope that you have a wonderful evening in exploring this wonderful new facility.[31] We also hope that you will come back here often in the future. At this time, I would like to introduce my investment partner in this park, Will Jerome."

"Good evening, ladies and gentlemen. I, too, would like to welcome all of you to this exceptional park. What a great way to celebrate the marriage of two very special people. Our groom, Keith Duggan, is the primary architect who designed this exciting new park. Fabulous work, Keith!" A spontaneous round of spirited applause showed that the assemblage agreed about the outstanding work Keith had done.

"And Miss Macie, our wonderful bride, now Mrs. Keith Duggan. Macie is a key member of my staff. I fully believe that she is destined to become a wonderful attorney someday. She has just recently been accepted for admission into the University of Minnesota law school." A spirited round of applause then sounded for the bride. "At this time, I 'd like to invite the newlyweds to the dance floor for their first dance." Keith took Macie's hand and led her to the center of the floor as boisterous applause sounded thru the pavilion. "Maestro…"

As the newlyweds started to waltz to the lovely orchestral music, Macie whispered to Keith. "I love you, Keith."

"I love you more, Macie."

They moved beautifully together in each other's arms, enjoying the wonder of the moment. The wedding party erupted in applause again as Keith bowed before his bride at the dance's conclusion.

"I didn't know there would be such a nice place for dancing. What fun it is here on 'our' island," Macie smiled with a sly grin.

Keith replied proudly. "This pavilion can hold up to 1,000 people. And it's scheduled to host many top orchestras and singers in the years to come."

Then, the Maestro encouraged the rest of the wedding party to join the newlyweds on the floor. Soon the newlyweds were surrounded by key friends, the Olsons, Seversons, Jeromes and Greenfields.

Later, during an intermission in the dancing, Keith invited the wedding party to follow him in a private tour of the new park.

On the formal paved walkway, Macie couldn't help noticing what her wedding guests were wearing -- women attired in full skirts and petticoats with pretty frilly white crinoline blouses or formal dresses of taffeta or tulle. Some wore smaller hats for the occasion. "White is in," Macie noticed. The men wore their best pale linen suits and bow ties.

Keith headed first for the Electric Tower. He explained how he designed it in Spanish Mission style mindful of an actual tower in Seville, Spain. Rising to 200 feet, it served as a water tower but mainly as a bold centerpiece for the new park. The tower was clad with hundreds of electric lights, which, now that it was dark, were illuminated. To power the lights, he explained, they had run a cable from the mainland all the way out to the island. The lights lit up the whole scene, sparkling like magic over the lake and the forested setting.

Macie marveled as they walked along, headed for the amusements at the east end of the park. "Look at all the excitement you've created, Keith. I hear lots of 'oohhh's' and 'aaaahhhh's.' "

"Tomorrow on opening day, there will be hopefully thousands of people here. Mr. Jerome and Thomas Louden must be giddy with excitement. I know they were confident that the streetcar line plus the new streetcar boats were sure to bring visitors from all over the Midwest to Big Island Park."

Then, turning to face his wedding party again, he continued: "This broad-looking building that we're passing on the left is the picnic pavilion. The path over there," he said, pointing to the right, "leads to the Merry Maze, a carousel, and an

Old Mill ride. I would encourage you to go try them out. And this path to the left leads down to an aviary and aquarium. There is so much to see and do here!"

Keith now led the group to the site of a stagecoach. Keith turned and explained to his party. "Well, folks. Macie and I are going to step into this stagecoach that will take us on our honeymoon trip to Yellowstone! Macie," Keith said, reaching out to take his bride's hand to usher her aboard the stagecoach. Once seated, Keith hollered in a voice loud enough for those outside the coach to hear: "Whoopie, Ti Yi Yo! Git along, little dogies!" Then, off they went in the simulated stagecoach, bouncing up and down as a short movie played within showing key sights from Yellowstone National Park.

"That was so fun!" Macie announced to her party as she stepped out of the coach. "You all must come back here later tonight to try it!"

Keith then led the group back to the pavilion for dinner and more dancing.

At the close of the evening, Keith and Macie went for a ride on the rollercoaster. It stopped unexpectedly midway through the course. Keith took Macie's hands in his, and in his tenderest voice said, "Macie, this has been the most wonderful day! I'm just so happy to be starting our new life together. I have a little surprise for you. While the stagecoach ride to Yellowstone was fun, would you be game to take a real honeymoon trip to New Orleans, the fabulous city where Meranda was raised?" Just as she was about to reply, the coaster took off again and the two were bounced back into their seats. Macie reached again for Keith's hands yelling," Yes! Yes!! YES!!" After the coaster came to a final stop, they disembarked and sat down nearby on a bench overlooking the lake. They both felt on top of the world as they cuddled together over the lake they knew so well.

A 1907 postcard of the Big Island Park wharves ferry landing.
Courtesy of the Excelsior Lake Minnetonka Historical Society

A path, as it exists today, that led to park amusements. The concrete path is cracked and worn.

Photo courtesy of Maritime Heritage Minnesota

Remains of an archway that surrounded the roller coaster area. *Photo courtesy of Maritime Heritage Minnesota*

Remains of roller coaster supports.
Photo courtesy of Maritime Heritage Minnesota

Acknowledgements

Thank you very much for reading our book! We hope that you enjoyed Big Island Remembered. We certainly had fun collaborating while writing it!

We would greatly appreciate your willingness to review our book on Amazon.com. In fact, you would make our day!

Thanks again!

Bette & Reed

We wish to thank the following people for their significant contributions to this book.

From Bette:
About six years ago I was reading about a St. Louis attorney who

figured prominently in Lake Minnetonka's history. I was very struck by his biography. Moreover, I decided that I'd like to write a mystery someday about the lake using this man as a leading character. Each of the people below have played important roles in helping this mystery to become a reality.

My daughter, Susan Hammel, as my only child, is a well-known entrepreneur in the financial world as a "philosophy major who went to Wall Street." She is of number one importance in my life, as my loving and trusted friend and caregiver. As a proficient reader, she has always supported me through my ups and downs in writing six books. She encouraged me to write this book and she reviewed an early draft, providing supportive yet critical feedback.

Susan's children, my granddaughter, Caleigh Hammel

Joyce and my grandson, Danny Hammel Joyce, insisted that even at 94, I was up to the task of tackling this latest book, my first try at writing fiction.

My New York daughter, (technically my stepdaughter), Anne Hammel, reviewed a late draft of the book and provided a wealth of valuable feedback and suggestions.

Last year after deciding to write this book, I enlisted my computer expert friend, Reed Wahlberg, to help me with the plot. We soon teamed up and Reed rapidly came into his own as a terrific writer.

My best friend, Peggy Watson, a voracious reader of fiction and non-fiction who is active in support of public libraries, provided a variety of excellent feedback after reading a late edition of the book.

I especially want to thank our editor, Ingrid Sundstrom Lundegaard, for her unfailing guidance of our manuscript. As a former Star & Tribune writer/editor, she quickly pointed out ways to improve certain chapters, quicken the pace and add more colorful details. Thanks to her initial reaction, we were inspired to do our best. That our completed script was written to her enthusiastic satisfaction was extremely rewarding.

From Reed:
Diane Meier, my wife, was instrumental in making this book a reality. Her support for the whole project never wavered. She was always ready to discuss ideas surrounding the story – usually in the middle of the night. She reviewed the entire book in detail and provided excellent feedback. Her work as a pediatrician continued, keeping our family financially afloat, while I ventured into the unknown in this crazy but fulfilling retirement activity. I am forever indebted for

her love and her support. This book is just the latest example in which Diane has contributed immeasurably to the quality of my life.

Pearl Meier, my mother-in-law, helped greatly throughout the creation of this book. She combed through her vast genealogical library for photos that could be used to illustrate the time period covered by our story. She contributed many ideas that were adopted into our plot. For example, the Bells chapter in our story is based on practices of the small town in rural Wisconsin where she grew up. Given that Pearl is suffering from macular degeneration, I read a later draft of the entire book aloud to Pearl. During that process, she provided critical feedback and, more importantly, she displayed boundless enthusiasm for the whole story that provided a key source of the energy required to complete this huge project. For my part, I dedicate this book to Pearl.

I thank my parents, Chuck and Isabelle Wahlberg, for their encouragement in all my life's endeavors. They were both avid readers who instilled in their offspring an appreciation for good books. I am forever grateful for their influence. My only regret is that my mother did not live to read this book. I know that she would have thoroughly enjoyed it.

Brian Peterson, attorney (and great Pickleball friend), provided critical feedback on the legal aspects of our story. Retired accountant Jerry Shaw provided helpful insights on characters in the story.

Paul Maravelas from the Minnesota Veterinary Historical Museum provided information about the role and prevalence of veterinarians in the era covered by our story.

Dawn Anderson did a very detailed review of a late draft of the book and offered many outstanding suggestions and corrections. She also gave us access to her extensive archive of beautiful photographs of Minnesota lakes, one of which we feature on our book cover.

Ann Merriman and Christopher Olson of Maritime Heritage Minnesota have conducted extensive archeological research on and around Big Island. They gave us unfettered access to their research reports and several of their photos are featured late in the book.

To Bette Hammel, my co-author, I extend my most sincere thanks. Bette is a professional journalist and a veteran author. She was willing to take me under her wing in this exciting project. I am forever grateful for her willingness to collaborate with a rookie. In my opinion, we make a good team.

About the authors

Bette Hammel

Wayzata's Bette Hammel is a highly respected Twin Cities author whose books have highlighted some of the Twin Cities' best-designed homes and architectural standouts.

After studying journalism at the University of Minnesota, she had stints with General Mills, where she wrote Betty Crocker scripts for NBC radio, then acquired radio station experience as a writer and broadcaster in Indiana and upper New York. Returning to Minnesota, she joined the advertising agency business where she used her radio and TV background for a multitude of accounts during the next 25 years.

The focus of her career shifted when she married Richard Hammel, co-founder of HGA Architects and

Engineers, in 1953. After her husband's untimely death in 1986, she was asked by the firm to document its history. With that project under way, she learned the language of architecture. The result was her first book, <u>From Bauhaus to Bow Ties: HGA Celebrates 35 Years,</u> published in 1989. Four other books on architecture soon followed.

Now, at age 94, Hammel still has plenty to write about. "She has a lot of energy, and she's interested in everything," says Ellen Green, a former editor. Green says Hammel illuminates well-designed buildings and recognizes the spirit of the architects who designed them. "It's really pointing out you don't have to know everything about architecture to enjoy it," Green says. But architecture might have a rival in Hammel's heart: Lake Minnetonka, where she often sailed with her husband as members of the Minnetonka Yacht Club. In addition to the beauty of the lake, Hammel is enamored with its storied past. "The history is so fascinating," she says. It was that fascination with the history of the lake along with her desire to write a novel that inspired this book.

Reed Wahlberg

Wayzata's Reed Wahlberg brings a very different vocational background to this project. After graduating from St. Olaf College in Northfield, MN, he coached competitive swimming for the Northfield Swim Club and St. Olaf College, and he taught French at Northfield High School. After developing a variety of computer software for use with his swim teams, he shifted careers and went to work as a software engineer for UnitedHealth Group and then WebMD. In another career move, he combined his long-term interests in statistics and quality improvement and launched his own consulting firm. He led improvement projects for several Twin Cities companies and taught classes in design of experiments for companies in multiple industries. In the final phase of his career, he went back to the corporate world and served as a quality engineer for Boston Scientific. He is now retired.

Reed has published articles on competitive swimming and design of experiments, but this is his first book. He teamed up with Bette as she was finishing her previous book, her autobiography, <u>A Lifetime of Luck and Pluck: A Memoir</u>. He assisted her mainly with computer issues. After completing that book, she mentioned a long-held desire to write a cozy mystery based on historical fiction around Lake Minnetonka. That idea piqued Reed's interest and their partnership took off in earnest.

Development of the book

Sharing a Margarita while waiting out a snowstorm during a research trip to Excelsior

After revising content while
vacationing on Sanibel Island

Bibliography

Best, Joel. <u>Controlling vice: regulating brothel prostitution in St. Paul</u>. The Ohio State University, 1998.

Cherland-McCune, Lori, Sue Cherland-Lescarbeau and Lisa Cherland-Kendrick. <u>Royal C. Moore: The Man Who Built the Streetcar Boats</u>. St. Paul, MN: Beaver's Pond Press 2012.

Dillman, Daisy Ellen. <u>100 Years in Excelsior</u>. Excelsior, MN: Tonka Printing Co., 1976.

Dregni, Eric. <u>By the Waters of Minnetonka</u>; Minneapolis: University of Minnesota Press, 2014.

Ellis, Samuel E., Jerry Wilson Holl. <u>Picturesque Minnetonka</u>. Excelsior, MN: Excelsior-Lake Minnetonka Historical Society, 1974.

Hornung, Clarence P. Handbook of Early Advertising Art. New York: Dover Publications, Inc., 1956.

Hyde, William, Howard Louis Conard. Encyclopedia of the history of St. Louis: a compendium of history and biography for ready reference. Volume 4. The Southern History Company, 1899. Available at: Link to book

Hallemann, Dave. Adoptions - Jefferson County, Missouri. Jefferson County Historical Society, 2001. Available at: http://jeffcomohistory.org/Adoptions_new.htm

Holst, Joanie (Wayzata Historical Society), Lisa Stevens (Excelsior-Lake Minnetonka Historical Society), Elizabeth Vandam (Westonka Historical Society). Lake Minnetonka, Images of America.

Charleston, SC: Arcadia Publishing, 2015.

Johnson, Frederick L. <u>The Big Water</u>. Deep Haven Books, 2012.

Jones, Thelma. <u>Once Upon A Lake</u>. Minneapolis: Ross and Haines, Inc., 1974.

Kunz, Virginia Brainard. <u>Minnetonka Yacht Club, Centennial 1882-1982.</u> Deephaven, MN: Minnetonka Yacht Club Sailing School. First edition, 1982.

Limbaugh, Rush. <u>The Adoption of Children in Missouri</u>, The, 2 MO. L. REV. (1937). Available at: https://scholarship.law.missouri.edu/mlr/vol2/iss3/2

Lowry, Goodrich. <u>Streetcar Man: Tom Lowry and the Twin City Rapid Transit Company</u>. Minneapolis: Lerner Publishing Group, 1979.

McCann, Dennis. <u>This Storied River. Legend & Lore of the Upper Mississippi</u>. Madison, WI: Wisconsin Historical Society Press, 2017.

McGinnis, Scott D., <u>Excelsior's waterfront. The history of the Excelsior Commons and Excelsior docks.</u> Chaska, MN: Scott D. McGinnis, 2008.

Meyer, Ellen Wilson. <u>Happenings Around Excelsior, The First Hundred Years, 1853-1953.</u> Excelsior, MN: Tonka Printing Company, 1982.

Meyer, Ellen Wilson. <u>Lake Minnetonka's Historic Hotels.</u> Excelsior, MN: Excelsior-Lake Minnetonka Historical Society. First edition, 1997.

Meyer, Ellen Wilson. <u>Picturesque Deephaven</u>. Excelsior, MN: Excelsior-

Lake Minnetonka Historical Society, 1989.

Ogland, James W. <u>Lake Minnetonka Historic Insights</u>. Wayzata, MN: DNALGO Publications, 2010.

Ogland, James W. <u>Picturing Lake Minnetonka, A Postcard History</u>. Minnesota Historical Society Press, 2001.

Peck, Grace A. <u>Excelsior Volunteer Fire Department: the early history : 1893-1993, one hundred years</u>. Excelsior, MN: Tonka Printing Company, 1993.

Robinson, Louis N. <u>Jails. Care and Treatment of Misdemeanant Prisoners in the United States</u>. Philadelphia: The John C. Winston Company, 1944.

Sykora, Barbara McHenry. "Charles Gibson's Lake Minnetonka

Summers." <u>Hennepin History Magazine</u>. Fall, 2013: 17 – 35.

Tollefson, Alan. <u>Shaping Our Community</u>. Excelsior, MN: Smith Printing, 2016.

Trenery, Walter. <u>Murder in Minnesota</u>. St. Paul: Minnesota Historical Society, 1962.

Twain, Mark. Neider, Charles, editor. <u>Complete Short Stories of Mark Twain.</u> New York: Bantam Classic, 2005.

Vandam, Elizabeth A. <u>Harry Wild Jones: American Architect.</u> Minneapolis: Nodin Press, 2008.

Endnotes

[1] Charles Gibson was a prominent St. Louis attorney during the latter portion of the 19th century. He is the historical figure loosely providing the inspiration for Will Jerome in our story. People in St. Louis started calling Charles Gibson "Sir Charles" in recognition of the work he did for leaders of Austria-Hungary and Prussia and the honors those leaders bestowed on him.

[2] The term 'black' for people of African origin was not commonly used during the period covered by this book. However, given that the term used at that time is considered so offensive today, it is not being used in this story.

[3] Illustrations found at the end of many of the chapters are taken copyright free from Clarence P. Hornung, <u>Handbook of Early Advertising Art</u>. (New York: Dover Publications, Inc., 1956).

[4] Dennis McCann, <u>This Storied River. Legend & Lore of the Upper Mississippi</u>. (Madison, WI: Wisconsin Historical Society Press, 2017), 103.

[5] To make muzzleloader ammunition during the Civil War, little droplets of lead were poured from the top of a tower, the droplets cooling and forming into balls as they fell into a vat of water. For more information, see <u>https://www.cityofdubuque.org/712/Shot-Tower</u>

[6] See https://en.wikipedia.org/wiki/Snake_Alley_(Burlington,_Iowa)

[7] This lock and dam actually opened about 14 years later. See https://en.wikipedia.org/wiki/Lock_and_Dam_No._19

[8] Thelma Jones, Once Upon A Lake. (Minneapolis: Ross and Haines, Inc., 1974) 249.

[9] We have taken some liberties here with the unreferenced account by Thelma Jones, p. 267. She reports that people saw 40-50 of Mr. Gibson's black hotel workers walking from the stop in Minnetonka Mills. Other sources like Frederick Johnson in The Big Water (Deep Haven Books, 2012) p. 56, mention that while Gibson inherited slaves, he led the effort to keep Missouri a free state

during the Civil War and he was known to have treated his black workers well.

[10] Jones, 249.

[11] Jones, 279.

[12] The character Ella Severson in our story is loosely based on the historical figure Ella Stratton. She was accorded the title "clerk for life" of the Congregational Church but we have chosen to make the Trinity Episcopal Church the center of our story. See Daisy Ellen Dillman. <u>100 Years in Excelsior</u>. (Excelsior, MN: Tonka Printing Co., 1976).

[13] Babbs Iger in our story is modeled after the historical figure, Babbs Ice. The details about the character in this chapter are factual. For more information, see Alan

Tollefson. <u>Shaping Our Community</u>. (Excelsior, MN: Smith Printing, 2016), 69.

[14] The following article appeared in the Excelsior Cottager on December 11, 1896:

> *Fires have been so numerous and the effects so destructive in this village that when a bell peals out on the frosty air in the night time, it brings every hearer to his feet, and as the cold sweat breaks out all over his body, he hastily dons clothing and rushes out to the scene of action. The ringing of the schoolhouse bell last Monday night was a false alarm, but it made people's hair stand just the same. Two boys, old enough to know better, broke into the building on the night mentioned, and passing through*

Miss Stratton's room where they struck a match, went to the hallway and tied a forty-foot rope to the bell-cord, leaving one end of the rope hanging out of the window. Then getting on the outside they gave the rope a few vigorous yanks and took to their heels, but not soon enough to hide their identity, and when wanted, they can be located. Besides placing themselves in a very unpleasant position, the boys are out a good 40-foot rope, which they can get by applying to the janitor of the school house."

Grace A. Peck. Excelsior Volunteer Fire Department: the early history : 1893-1993, one hundred years. Excelsior, MN: Tonka Printing Company, 1993, p. 18.

[15] The character of Thomas Louden in our story is loosely based on the historical figure, Thomas Lowry. For more information, see Goodrich Lowry. <u>Streetcar Man: Tom Lowry and the Twin City Rapid Transit Company</u>. (Minneapolis: Lerner Publishing Group, 1979).

[16] For more on "How came you so" and other idiomatic expressions of the 1800's, see <u>https://www.npr.org/sections/npr-history-dept/2015/07/21/423297371/12-lost-american-slangisms-from-the-1800s</u>.

[17] Flash photography was in its infancy at this time but it is probably a little early for photographs to have been printed in the Excelsior newspaper.

[18] The City Beautiful Movement was a reform philosophy of architecture and urban planning that flourished during the 1890s and 1900s with the intent of introducing beautification and monumental grandeur in major U.S. cities. See https://en.wikipedia.org/wiki/City_Beautiful_movement. Leroy Buffington was a very prominent architect at this time and a proponent of this movement. See https://en.wikipedia.org/wiki/Leroy_Buffington.

[19] According to procedures in Minnesota at the time of this story, when a person was found dead as a likely result of violence, the county coroner would hold an inquest. A jury of six people would view the body, hear from any witnesses, and reach a verdict about the likely cause of death. If a suspect was identified,

that person could be arrested. If no suspect was immediately identified, the local law enforcement officer would initiate an investigation. For more information, see Walter Trenery. <u>Murder in Minnesota</u> (St. Paul: Minnesota Historical Society, 1962) 227.

[20] The Pillsbury family did not establish their home on the lake until later in the 20th century.

[21] Including a reference to Mr. Jimmy in our story is our largest stretch in historical timeline. Any fan of 1960s rock 'n roll or the Rolling Stones is encouraged to consult the Internet for the folkloric story about Excelsior's "roving ambassador," his encounter with Mick Jagger and the song "You Can't Always Get What You Want."

[22] The White House was in operation from 1872–1946. It featured a good kitchen and a large porch overlooking the bay. James Ogland. <u>Lake Minnetonka Historic Insights</u>. (Wayzata, MN: DNALGO Publications, 2010), 36.

[23] For more information see Lori Cherland-McCune, et al., <u>Royal C. Moore: The Man Who Built the Streetcar Boats</u>. (St. Paul, MN: Beaver's Pond Press, 2012).

[24] Historical note: the trolley line to Excelsior did not open until something like 1906.

[25] Historical note: the new capitol building opened in 1905.

[26] The story told about Louise Robinson of St. Paul in this book is largely based on historical fact

although the name of the historical figure was Mary Robinson. For more information, see Joel Best, <u>Controlling Vice: Regulating Brothel Prostitution in St. Paul, 1865–1883</u>. (The Ohio State University, 1998). Some of the details have been modified for our story. Meranda Delaquila is a totally fictious character with no link to the real Mary Robinson.

[27] An experience by co-author Reed inspired the use of the nugget in our story. Reed's maternal grandfather mined for gold in the Highlands near Butte, Montana. Reed often heard stories during his childhood about the mineshaft, the cabin that his mom's family built and frequented, and their many adventures in the Highlands. Reed, his wife, Diane, and their eight-year-old son, Nathaniel, decided to try to find the cabin and the mineshaft during a

vacation out west. To locate the site, Reed's mom had told them to talk with the resident miner, Howard Stratton, whose homestead was located along the small road winding through the Highlands. Reed's family did indeed find Howard and his wife and they had a great discussion about mining and encounters with Reed's grandparents. During that discussion, Howard told them about the incredible nugget that that he and his son had found. He also showed them a picture of it. It can be viewed on the Internet by searching for 'Highland Centennial Nugget.' A picture of Howard holding his nugget can be seen on Facebook. Howard did successfully guide Reed's family to the creek bed leading to the old cabin and mineshaft. They found the site after a steep one-mile hike up the mountain. What fun it was to find and explore the source of so much family lore!

[28] For more information on St. Mary's see William Hyde & Howard Louis Conard. Encyclopedia of the history of St. Louis: a compendium of history and biography for ready reference. Volume 4. (The Southern History Company, 1899), pp. 1975-1976.

[29] See Dave Hallemann, <u>Adoptions - Jefferson County, Missouri</u>. (Jefferson County Historical Society, 2001) Available at: http://jeffcomohistory.org/Adoptions_new.htm

[30] Jails of the period were often under complete control of the local sheriff. Prisoners were often held for long periods of time while awaiting trial. Over 40% of prisoners in that

era were held there due to disorderly conduct and drunkenness. Louis Robinson. <u>Jails. Care and Treatment of Misdemeanant Prisoners in the United States</u>. (Philadelphia: The John C. Winston Company, 1944), 26 & 44.

[31] The park actually opened in 1906. The historical figure, attorney Charles Gibson (Will Jerome in this story), played no role in Big Island park. He had died in 1899.

Made in the USA
Monee, IL
30 July 2020